D1352176

LEPRECHAUN'S GOLD

When Maggie Nolan runs back home to Ireland after an unhappy love affair, she finds enough trouble to engulf her. Her father blames the handsome stranger Maggie met in the storm, but Adam Blair is the only person who can help. The trouble is, Maggie is plunged into a morass of lies and deceit. Even worse, she realizes that she has fallen in love with a man whom her father disapproves of and whom, it appears, is still in love with his wife.

DINA McCALL

♦

LEPRECHAUN'S GOLD

Complete and Unabridged

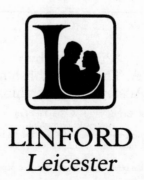

LINFORD
Leicester

First published in Great Britain

First Linford Edition
published 2002

British Library CIP Data

McCall, Dina
    Leprechaun's gold.—Large print ed.—
Linford romance library
1. Love stories
2. Large type books
I. Title
823.9'14 [F]

ISBN 0–7089–9833–X

Published by
F. A. Thorpe (Publishing)
Anstey, Leicestershire

Set by Words & Graphics Ltd.
Anstey, Leicestershire
Printed and bound in Great Britain by
T. J. International Ltd., Padstow, Cornwall

This book is printed on acid-free paper

1

Maggie Nolan was running away. That's how some people might have seen it, but she didn't care. She was going home. The thought had helped during the rough ferry crossing from Fishguard to Rosslare, and it kept her going now as she drove her Mini over roads slick with mud. The windscreen wipers moving jerkily backwards and forwards were having a hard time clearing the rivers of rain, and the light was fading fast, but from here on she would have no trouble finding her way. Hadn't she travelled these roads often enough in Da's old truck, taking the produce of the smallholding to Duncow market? It was ironic. She had fought so hard to get away from Ballybrae; now every moment was taking her back — and she was glad.

She leaned forward to wipe the inside

of the misted windscreen. The heater wasn't working, but the car hadn't been a bad buy, considering how little she'd spent on it. It was the only good thing she had acquired during her time in London. Everything else had been loss. Yes . . . it was time she went home.

Besides which, Da would be glad to have her back. Maggie changed down a gear as she negotiated a tricky corner. Her wide forehead creased in a thoughtful frown as she recalled how her father's letters had been few and far between. Regrettably her visits back to him had been widely spaced too. Although he said he was getting on 'famously' she guessed he hated living alone. But there was something worse than that, something wrong. She had sensed it for some time, without being able to put her finger on it.

'Jeez!'

Headlights dazzled her and she blinked, stabbing her foot on the brake. The car slewed drunkenly to one side. Something large loomed up, and she clawed frantically at the wheel, over-compensating. The Mini slithered sideways. It lurched — righted itself — lurched again, tilted sickeningly, and stopped with a thump. She was thrown hard against the restraint of her seat-belt. Then the engine cut out.

It was pitch black now, with nothing to be heard except the drumming of rain on the car roof. Maggie fought the desire to burst into tears. Slowly her fingers relaxed on the steering wheel. Her heart was still pounding but, with the initial fright over, a new thought was beginning to assert itself.

'Wouldn't you know it?' she breathed in despair. 'I'm in the blasted ditch.'

She released her seat-belt and switched off the ignition. What should she do? Stay like this all night . . . in which case her father would be worried sick, because he was expecting her . . . or walk the remaining miles to Ballybrae, and catch her death of pneumonia? She didn't fancy either, but it might be as well to see if she *could* open her door. The handle turned easily enough, and the door opened a crack, just enough to let the rain drive in, but that was as far as it would go. Slithering around, she bent up her knees and got her feet on the passenger seat; that way she could get her shoulder against the door. Then it was wrenched open. Maggie gave a yelp of fright.

'Are you all right?' She could only just hear the man's voice through the wind and the rain that gusted in with it. Of course . . . she had quite forgotten about the other car.

'I think so,' she shouted, her voice snatched away by the wind. She started to wriggle through the opening, the rain taking her breath, when his hand took hold of her collar, and with a jerk that nearly throttled her he yanked her clear of the car. She staggered as her feet touched the ground, and found herself clasped hard against him. Her nose was buried in a soft wet anorak, but beneath the clothing she could feel the strength of his body. My God . . . he must be strong, to lift her out like that — she was by no means tiny!

She screwed up her eyes against the rain as the dark figure bent down to speak, his breath warm in her ear. 'You'd better get into the Land Rover. There's nothing we can do in this.' Maggie's breath caught in her throat. The depth of his voice confirmed her impression of strength, but more than that, to her surprise — alarm even — it vibrated deep inside her, as if something there responded. The feeling was not altogether pleasant, but she had no time to analyze it as he hurried her to his vehicle, his arm around her shoulders steadying her. He hoisted Maggie into the passenger seat. For a moment, as she sat alone, she felt strangely insecure. The hands that had manhandled her so roughly had at least felt safe and warm. Then, to her relief, he ran around to the driver's side and climbed in. Maggie pushed her wet hair away from her face.

He slammed shut his door. 'Well — aren't you going to say it?'

That deep voice again! It was unsettling. She didn't care for what it was doing to her, at all. It was like when she first met Malcolm . . . only much much worse. She was over all that kind of thing, and even if she wasn't this was hardly the time for it. She turned reluctantly to look at him, but he was only a dark anonymous mass in the seat beside her . . . a bulky man, judging from the space he filled.

'Am I not going to say what?' she asked stiffly.

'That it was my fault. That my lights dazzled you, and I shouldn't have had them on main beam.'

If it was an apology it was a strange back-handed one, but disarming, as no doubt he had intended it to be. In the darkness her generous lips curved into a smile, and the smile somehow crept into her voice. 'You seem to have said it all for me. There's nothing for me to add . . . unless you're hoping I'll contradict you!'

He chuckled. 'No. My excuse is that I wasn't expecting any traffic on this road. Are you on your way to see Mr Nolan?'

He's English, she thought. And fairly strange to these parts. Only a stranger would speak of Da so formally. Her father was Bonnie to those who knew him — and that was nearly everybody.

'I am,' she agreed. Then defiantly, ' . . . or rather I was, until you forced me off the road.'

'There was plenty of room for both us,' he objected calmly. 'If you hadn't over-reacted.'

'If you hadn't blinded me I wouldn't have needed to react.'

'Well . . . you have a point there.' He ended the argument by starting up the engine.

His laconic manner, and the effect his voice had on her made Maggie feel perverse. 'Hold on a minute! What about my car?'

'I'll have it pulled out in the

morning.' She saw what he meant. He couldn't do anything in this wind and rain. Nevertheless, she persisted, hardening her heart. 'My suitcases are in the boot. It was your fault. I think the least you can do is to get my things. Here are the keys.'

He groaned. 'Oh . . . very well.' She got the impression that he was not really all that put out. He switched on the interior light, and she saw she had been right. He *was* a big man, appearing more so because of his bulky anorak. The face so close to hers was strong and square with a forceful chin . . . an austere face, with hooded eyes and thick brown hair made unruly by the wind. As he took the keys from her, his fingers brushed warm against her own, sending a shock through her system. For what seemed an eternity their eyes locked . . . then he tossed the keys up and caught them again. 'I'll be back in a tick.' He was gone, leaving her with the memory of a quick unexpected smile that brought his face alive, and a fluttering in the pit of her stomach she could not account for. Reaction, she supposed.

Maggie shivered, and pulled her jacket closer. Feeling in her pocket she found a handkerchief and wiped the rain from her face. He had looked nice, she admitted — well, more than nice, perhaps — from the brief glimpse she had had of him, and he had been right. She hadn't handled her car very well . . . but in her defence it must be said that she had never had such a fright before. She wondered what his business was with her Da. He must have come from Ballybrae, because the road — more of a track really — led nowhere else.

He returned, flinging her cases into the back of the Land Rover, and shaking the rain from himself like a large shaggy dog.

'Thank you,' she said, in a voice carefully noncommittal. They drove on in total silence. He made her feel uneasy. She was too completely aware of him . . . of the smell of wet anorak and aftershave . . . of his knuckles brushing her knee when he changed gear. After all, what did she know about him? He could be anyone — a mass murderer — a rapist . . .

'Are you always like this?' he asked.

Maggie jumped. 'What d'you mean?'

'So calm. Most women would have been crying.' His voice was icy with contempt for a moment, as if he didn't think very much of most women. 'They'd be screaming and having hysterics. But not you. Are you always a quiet one?'

Maggie laughed out loud then. If only he knew what she had been thinking! 'Maybe you know the wrong women,' she ventured.

'You could be right at that.' A bleakness had crept into his voice, as if for the moment he had forgotten all about her. She wondered with interest if she had said the wrong thing . . . touched on a sore spot, perhaps. He was a man women would seek out, she

10

had seen enough to know that, but she had learned not to be disturbed by handsome men . . . or hoped she had!

'Now that *was* a typical chauvinist remark,' she said, in an effort to pull herself together. 'Women can be just as sensible as men . . . more so, indeed.'

'They certainly know how to get their own way,' he commented drily. 'Look at you — sending me to my death in that rain.'

'I doubt you'll have come to much harm,' she said, amused. He had a sense of humour after all. She liked that. Malcolm had been rather short on humour, she remembered. 'I'll keep your keys and have the car brought up in the morning,' he said. 'If there's any damage I'll see that it's made good.'

'That's kind of you.'

'It's the least I can do.' He hesitated. 'So . . . you're going up to Ballybrae. Are you a relation of Mr Nolan's?'

'I'm Maggie Nolan.'

'His daughter?' He sounded cautious. Now, that was strange, for he did not

11

seem a cautious man — far too sure of himself for that.

'I've heard of you,' he continued. 'How you struggled to leave here. Learned shorthand and typing . . . and off you went.'

She relaxed, staring at the sheets of rain travelling down the side window. 'After mother died I couldn't wait to be away. I thought life must be so much more exciting over the water.'

He gave a short laugh. 'The grass is always greener . . . isn't that always the way with women? And did you find the streets of London paved with gold?'

''Deed I did . . . leprechaun's gold,' she answered softly.

'I beg your pardon?'

'Oh! . . . ' Maggie laughed at herself for having spoken her thoughts aloud. 'Haven't you heard the stories? You know . . . about how, when you find a leprechaun's pot of gold, in the morning the coins have turned to dirty old pebbles.'

'Poor Maggie! A man, I suppose?'

He shifted in his seat, and she got the impression he was glancing down at her hands in the dim light of the instrument panel. Aware of the squareness of her long capable fingers, she folded them neatly on her lap.

'So what went wrong?'

'I found out he was married.' She gave the fact baldly, with no excuses or explanation.

'I see.' He weighed the information. 'And this made a difference?'

'Well . . . naturally.' Maggie's voice had risen, but then she stopped, abashed. 'I . . . oh, you won't be wanting to hear all that!'

He took his time before answering. 'You interest me. Few women I know would draw back from an affair, just because the man was married. It would probably make them all the keener.'

'You're very cynical,' she objected. 'Marriage is important.'

'You're a rare bird.'

After that he said no more, and she sat in the dark beside him, her mind jolted into wandering back over the last few years. It had been the old, old tale. Surely, to fall for one's boss must be the ultimate in bad jokes, and to find out, too late, that he was married had only made it worse. It had never even occurred to her to ask. That showed how naïve she had been. When she had walked into Malcolm's office, proud of her newly-acquired business diplomas, she must have seemed a sitting duck. How everyone must have laughed . . . though Malcolm had been careful to keep their affair discreet. Too discreet. Maggie's mouth twisted wryly. 'Deed . . . that should have warned her!

The thing that angered her most had been his bland assumption that when she did find out about his wife, she would accept the situation. 'It needn't make any difference to us, darling!' She could still see his face . . . smiling . . . confident. 'It doesn't matter.'

'It matters to *me*!' she had told him firmly. Then, with as much dignity as she could muster, she had handed in her notice.

At first she had thought of other jobs. After working for Malcolm, she was well enough qualified at twenty-five to start afresh. But something called her back. That was why she was heading for Ballybrae, where it was not considered gauche to have principles.

Would she still be with Malcolm, if he had been free? The thought did not bring any leaping of the pulse, any feeling of regret. Had she really been in love with him after all, or had the strong wine of freedom gone to her head? She was still pondering this, as they drew up in the yard at Ballybrae.

The outside light was on, showing she was expected, and the rain had eased to a mere drizzle. Her companion deposited her cases near the doorway to the house. He stood beside her like a rock, the wind blowing his hair over his forehead, and held out his hand. 'I'll be seeing you again, Maggie Nolan.' It was a statement of fact.

'Yes,' she answered gravely, placing her hand in his. He nodded, as though an important question had been answered. The warmth from his fingers sent a tingling of gooseflesh right up her arm and into her shoulders. Her skin had taken on a new sensitivity. She could feel the firm smoothness of his palm against hers, and the sensation threw her right off balance.

'I don't even know your name,' she remarked, to break the bemused feeling that had gripped her. It was not like her to be fanciful. She had considered herself to be down to earth, able to make sensible considered decisions — and yet she had learned absolutely nothing about this man, while he now knew more than enough about her! One thing she was sure of, though . . . she wanted to know him better.

'Adam Blair.' He sounded as if he expected it to mean something to her, but it didn't. He was still holding her hand, and she tried to withdraw it, but his fingers tightened. His eyes still held hers, inscrutable under the heavy lids. His face was stern, the lines sharpened by the night's shadows. Without any conscious volition on her part Maggie found herself swaying towards him as though mesmerized. Then the cottage door opened, spilling a bright shaft of light across the yard.

'Maggie? Is that you?'

With a gasp of relief, she tore her hand away. 'Da! Oh, it's good to see you.'

'Maggie, me little girl . . . give your owd Da a kiss!'

She hugged him, warmed by his welcome, but at the same time surprised at how much smaller he seemed. He stiffened.

'Mr Blair . . . is that you, Sorr?'

'Yes, Nolan. I'm off now . . . I'll be seeing you.'

'Aye, aye . . . no doubt you will. No doubt you will.'

Her father pushed her through the doorway, muttering under his breath. She looked back to thank Adam again, but he was leaving and she closed the door with a pang of regret.

'Come on in now, child. My, you're wet . . .'

Her father busied himself at the fire, which would not have warmed a cat, so low had it burned. He poked the end of a pair of bellows through the bars of the grate, puffing the flames into life. Maggie looked around her with dismay. The signs of neglect were all too apparent. True, the room was much as when she had left. The square wooden table was still covered by the red chenille cloth that hung nearly to the floor, but on it were the remains of past meals. The heavy oak sideboard still housed the photographs of her late mother and herself as a child — but they were almost buried in mounds of untidy paperwork, and dust lay everywhere.

'I'd have prepared a dish of something,' Bonnie Nolan puffed at the fire. 'But I just sat down . . . and would you believe it, I fell asleep.'

Maggie's cool gaze flickered around the room, and lit on the bottle of Irish standing on the floor, conveniently close to her father's favourite chair. 'Oh Da!' she whispered, reproachfully.

'I'm sorry,' he said, deliberately misunderstanding her. 'Shall I get you something now?'

'No . . . no! You get the fire going. I'll see what I can find.'

While her father held a newspaper over the grate to draw the flames, Maggie took off her jacket, shook the rain from it, placed it over the back of a chair, and then rolled up her sleeves. She was still wearing what she called her 'office clothes', a high-necked white blouse and straight black skirt, that gave her an efficient, almost severe, look. Her thick dark hair, drawn back into a knot at the nape of her neck, would have heightened the 'no nonsense' effect, had it not been for the fact that the wind and rain had caused tendrils to escape, curling around her temples. Even the plain blouse, tucked

19

so carefully in at the waist, could not disguise the fact that Maggie Nolan was all woman. She was tall, with a casual voluptuous grace, her mobile mouth intriguingly balanced by candid clear grey eyes ... eyes that were now looking around her with a worried expression, as she explored the kitchen cupboards.

'Have you been feeding yourself properly, Da?'

'What's that?'

She wandered back into the doorway, a basin with one lone egg in it in her hands. 'I said, have you been eating?'

Her father looked up. He was a small man, and she remembered him as being rounded and merry, but now those chubby cheeks were veined, and the blue eyes watery and wavering ... evasive.

'Eating? Well, of course I have. Oh, you mean there's not much there? Well now, I can explain that. You see, I haven't had time ... '

Maggie shook her head, and went

back to her foraging. She should never have left him! After her mother died she had been too full of her own plans, her schemes, her ambitions, to think clearly what it would mean. And her father — bless him — had encouraged her in what she now saw as her selfishness. 'Sure and you've studied all this time,' he had said. 'Your mother would have wanted you to make the most of your life. Away with you now. I'll be fine . . . just fine.'

She sighed, remembering. How immature she had been, to believe him. Without her mother's strength he was like a child himself.

'Well, you'll eat with me now,' she called cheerfully. *Or you will if I can find anything!* Then, coming across another egg, and crossing her fingers that neither would prove bad, she broke them both into a basin. Before long she had whipped up an omelette, eked out with a little chopped onion and tomato, and the grated remains of some hardened cheese. With great wedges of bread and butter, and a pot of tea, it would have to do until she could visit the shops. She loaded everything onto a tray and carried it back into the next room, where her father had cleared the table by the simple expedient of shifting the debris onto the already cluttered sideboard. The fire had burned up, the flames leaping to cast shadows on the walls.

'Isn't this a feast now!' exclaimed Bonnie Nolan. 'Sit you down, Maggie girl — you must be tired. Aren't I an unfeeling man, to make you work like this, and you only just home after all this time.'

He was buttering her up, she could sense his nervousness even if she could not understand it. 'Eat your food,' she scolded gently. 'It was high time I came home, I think.'

His eyes filled. 'I missed you, Maggie,' he said simply.

She reached across and held his hand. 'And I missed you Da.'

Later, when she had washed the

dishes and tidied away at least some of the clutter, they sat together in quiet companionship. Maggie stretched her long shapely legs out to the fire, luxuriating in its heat. Staring at the flames, she smiled secretly, thinking about that recent, strange drive through the dark. She wondered what Adam Blair might be . . . a farmer perhaps? He had a kind of rugged dependability about him. Whatever he did, she was sure he would excel at it; that unforgettable face would not be one to accept a subordinate role. Maggie wiggled her toes comfortably. Something about Adam Blair had reached out and touched her, and she was sure it had been the same for him, whoever he was. Soon she would ask Da about him, but that pleasure must keep. There were other things she had to sort out first. With an effort she roused herself.

'When did you last go to the market, then?'

Her father fidgetted. 'Oh — Tuesday I think it was . . . maybe.'

'And you didn't go to the shops while you were in town?'

'I . . . I was too busy.' He was lying, and she knew it. She leaned forward and touched his knee.

'Da, what is it? Haven't you been sending much to the market . . . is that it? Have the crops been poor?'

He rose, and began to pace the room. 'I . . . I haven't done too well, Maggie. It's been awful bad weather, and I've been too busy.'

'But I thought young Jimmy Connor was working for you? That was what we arranged when I went.'

'Oh — to be sure. He'll be along in the morning, but then there's the potatoes to get up. I'm not so young, Maggie. There's a lot to be done.'

She hated seeing him like this. Where was the all-powerful omnipotent father she had known? That was how he had appeared to the trustful eyes of a child, and she had still seen him in that light when she left. But now she was looking at him with the eyes of a woman. She should have come back to visit more often, she thought guiltily, but there had always been something to stop her. First it had simply been the lack of funds, then later it had been Malcolm . . .

'I'll give you a hand with the potatoes tomorrow,' she reassured him. 'We'll soon get them up.'

He gave a little smile. 'You're a good girl, Maggie.' He didn't seem any happier. A cold finger of unease touched her.

'You're not ill, are you Da?'

'Ill . . . me? Oh no . . . no, I'm fine — just fine.'

'That you're not! Da, will you stop traipsing up and down, and sit here and tell me what's wrong.'

He returned to his chair, and sat staring into the fire. His right hand groped on the floor beside him, and found the whiskey bottle. Pouring himself a stiff tot, he held the glass for a moment, and then tossed it back and poured another. 'I'm in a little bit of debt, that's all. It's nothing.' He took another gulp, and waved his other hand airily. 'I had a loan from the owd man. I was needing it for the fertilizer . . . and . . . and other things.'

Maggie was puzzled. The old man her father referred to was Seamus Monohan, owner of the rambling big house at the top of the hill, and landlord to the tenant farmers around, her father being one of them. It was the usual thing to take a loan from him to buy seed or stock — rather than bothering an unsympathetic bank manager. Mr Monohan preferred it that way. He had always looked after his tenants, and they respected him, speaking of him with affection. She knelt on the rug beside her father, and leaned against him. 'But I don't understand. You've had loans from the owd man before. There's never been any bother.'

An angry flush spread over Bonnie Nolan's face. He set his glass down with a bang that made the remaining whiskey spill. 'And there wouldn't be now, there would *not* . . . not if the owd man was alive and here, and not that black-hearted, tight-fisted . . . '

She picked on the few words she did understand. 'You mean, Seamus Monohan is dead? But Da, when was this? Why didn't you write and tell me?' She felt a stab of grief — not just for the old man — she had hardly known him, though as a child she had often run across his fields, and seen him walking. He had always waved to her. No . . . it was just one more thing to bring home to her how things had changed.

'Ah now, I'm not one for writing . . . you know that. And haven't I had more things on my mind since *he's* taken over . . . pestering me . . . telling me what to do . . . that, that . . . '

He spluttered with rage, and reached for the bottle once more. Maggie took it gently from his hand. 'Who are you talking about?'

Bonnie Nolan jumped up, and

resumed his jerky pacing. He waved his arms. 'That divil, that cold fish, that . . . foreigner! Adam Blair, that's who I'm talking about. The man who brought you here tonight.' He shot an agitated finger at his daughter. 'And you haven't explained what you were doing with the man. How come you arrived with him, that's what I'd like to know.'

Time froze, suspended, before Maggie could bring herself to speak. 'He gave me a lift, that's all,' she faltered. 'His lights dazzled me, and I landed in the ditch, so . . . '

'Ha!' her father crowed, triumphant. 'There you are, then! That's the sort of man he is. Not content with ruining me, doesn't he try to kill my daughter?'

'That's nonsense,' she said quietly. 'It was an accident. He was very helpful. I can't see what he has to do with having a loan from Seamus Monohan.'

He tutted with exasperation. 'Don't you listen at all? Isn't he the new owner of everything the owd man had? He's the only surviving male relative . . . a nephew, or something . . . from England. Now he comes threatening me . . . '

'Threatening you?' Her interruption was sharp. 'What d'you mean?'

'Aren't I telling you?' Bonnie Nolan's voice rose an octave. 'He's talking of taking the tenancy off me. Me, that's been here since I was born, and my father before me. I brought your mother here as a bride, and from here I buried her . . . '

He broke down, and Maggie scrambled to her feet to hold him to her. He buried his face in her shoulder, and she patted his back, murmuring — crooning almost as if he were a baby. 'Don't fret Da, don't take on so. I'll see him and explain things. I expect he doesn't realize how things were done here when his uncle was alive.'

But he'll soon find out! she thought indignantly, her lips tightly pressed together. To think she had liked the man. To think she had even thought . . . well, never mind about that now. It had been foolish, like a schoolgirl getting a crush over someone, and just because of a rich deep voice. She would never have imagined him the kind of person who would hound an old man over a few measly pounds! That must have been his business at Ballybrae that very evening. No wonder her father had been in such a state when she arrived. 'Don't worry, Da,' she said. 'Everything will be all right — I promise.'

After a while she managed to persuade her father to go to bed, and once she was left alone she tidied up as much as she could of the muddle in the kitchen, and retired to her room. It was cold in there. The only heating was by means of an old oil heater, and she was not sure where that was kept these days — or indeed whether her father had bought any paraffin — so she undressed hastily, and lost no time in pulling on a long white nightdress. Thank goodness she had not forgotten what it could be like at Ballybrae. She sat at the dressing-table, and undid her knot of hair. Unrestrained, it fell over her shoulders, and she brushed it with long easy strokes, the way she always had, the way her mother had trained her. Framing her face in a dark cloud, it quite changed her appearance. Gone was all the severity, the cool efficiency she had found it useful to assume. The image staring back at her from the mirror was that of an unsure and troubled girl with clouded eyes and a soft vulnerable mouth.

At last she finished and jumped into bed, tucking the blankets close about her. Gradually she became warm, but sleep eluded her, even though she felt exhausted. She tossed and turned. It was one thing to promise her father that all would be well . . . but could she really sort things out for him? Would Adam Blair listen to her?

He must! It wasn't her father's fault that things were bad. Surely even a man unused to country ways could see that.

She had a little money saved up; if they could get the produce flowing to the market again, business might pick up. Poor Da! She should never have left him. He was a good man — but weak. But as she drifted away, the emotion that gripped her above all others was bitter disappointment.

I really liked him, she thought. I really liked Adam Blair! Indeed, she had to admit it had been more than that. It was what she had been keeping safe inside her, to bring out and savour once she was alone — to examine, and wonder at, and perhaps hope about . . . until her father had shown her the kind of man Adam Blair really was.

It proved yet again what a fool she could be. First Malcolm, and now a perfect stranger! It was just as well she had discovered the truth — it might have stopped her getting into a lot more trouble.

2

A band of sunlight spilled through a gap in the curtains, crept across the heavy crocheted bedspread, and eventually reached Maggie's face. She made a moan of protest, and pulled the covers over her head. She had been comfortable — in a dream where a deep voice had been murmuring things she wanted to hear. She strained to retain the memory, but the dream slid beyond her grasp. She supposed she had been dreaming of Malcolm again — it was only natural, really. Outside, a dog barked. She gave a muffled sigh, and emerged bemused and tousled, to grope for her watch on the bedside cabinet.

The dog barked again. Throwing back the blankets she jumped out of bed and crossed to the window, bare feet cold on the flowered linoleum. The rain had stopped. Puddles in the yard showed the extent of the previous night's downpour, but now the sun shone, and the fields on the other side of the wall lay green under a clear sky. So green! She had forgotten just how beautiful a colour that could be. A black dog padded around a corner, and cocked its leg against the gate post. Following it came a young man — barely more than a boy. Maggie opened the window and leaned out.

'Jimmy . . . Jimmy Connor, is that you?'

He looked up and grinned. 'Maggie . . . you're back then?'

'As you can see! What are you doing?'

He shrugged. 'Lifting 'taties, I 'spect.'

'I'll be with you . . . give me a few minutes.' She snapped shut the window. She should have been ready and waiting to give a hand, as she had promised — a fine thing, to be laggardly this first morning!

In the bathroom the water ran cold. That was one of the things that had made her so keen to get away — the raw discomfort of a home where there had never been quite enough; never enough money, never enough warmth, never enough security. Maggie towelled herself vigorously, reflecting that she'd grown too soft. The centrally heated flesh-pots of London had made her forget the raw chill of an October morning in Ballybrae. It would be nice if they could install a more reliable hot water system than the ugly great boiler that lurked in the corner — but that wasn't likely, in debt as they were.

Adam Blair! She froze, staring at her reflection in the fly-specked mirror, her mouth round with horror. The man in her dream! A shiver ran down her spine. Why think of him, of all people . . . and in such a way? It was beginning to come back to her. There was no doubt about it, she remembered the dream-touch of his body against her own . . . and she had actually been enjoying it. She gasped as the details returned to her. Why — it was almost

. . . indecent! She flushed, and avoided her own gaze. She had not thought about a man in that way since Malcolm, and preferred not to remember *him*. But dreams were different. One couldn't be held responsible for dreams . . . so why feel guilty about this one? Forget it. It meant nothing.

Cursing herself for an overactive imagination, she almost ran back to the bedroom, and dragged from her still-unpacked cases a red checked shirt and a pair of black corduroy trousers. Pulling them up over sleekly rounded hips she put her mind to the predicament her father had landed them in. Not that he had done it deliberately, she thought loyally, but all the same, it was worrying. She tucked the shirt in at the waist, and fastened the buttons, while her mind searched for solutions. It was clear they must get some income flowing in, and that meant taking produce to the market. Although late in the year there ought to be enough to send a steady supply. That was how it had been in the past, and though — goodness knows — they had never become rich, they had never starved either.

Another minute, and with her hair dragged severely back and tied out of the way, she was down the stairs and rooting in the glory hole where the junk of past ages had accumulated. Sure enough, her gumboots were still there, buried under a discarded rug and a cardboard box of empty bottles. Her old red anorak, faded and torn, was hanging on its hook behind the back door. Slipping herself into its familiar warmth, she let herself out into the yard. Jimmy was in the barn, trying to start the tractor ... without much success, it appeared. Maggie leaned against it, her hands pushed deep into her pockets, and watched him. His fresh young skin, hardly yet needing the stroke of a razor, was pink with the morning cold. He was embarrassed, she realized, at being unable to start the beast, with her standing there.

'It's no good. It's been playing up all week, but now it's finally kicked the bucket. Sure, and it's only fit for the knacker's yard.' He jumped down, and kicked at one of its wheels in disgust.

Maggie looked around her. 'Where's Da?'

'I haven't seen him yet. I doubt he's up.' He gave her a sideways glance. 'He . . . he lies in sometimes.'

An awful suspicion held her. 'I'll be back,' she said, and turned to the house. Straight up the stairs she went, and rapped at her father's door. There was no answer, so she looked in. Bonnie Nolan lay in the sleep-tossed muddle of a big double bed, his mouth open, oblivious to the world, his clothes a discarded heap on the floor, an empty whiskey bottle nestling on the pillow beside his head. The room reeked of it.

'Da!' She shook him gently. He gave a grunt, and turned over, dragging the bed clothes with him. Her eyes stung as she stroked the faded thinning hair that showed above the blankets. What had brought her father to this state? Surely not simply Adam Blair — if it was she would have something to say to that man, dream or no dream.

When she rejoined Jimmy he still had not succeeded in bringing the tractor to life, and was standing disconsolately beside it. 'It's no good,' he said. 'Last time it was fixed Bonnie was told he was wasting his time. Anyway . . . it's ancient.'

He did not ask after her father, she noticed, as if the boy was used to it, and knew what to expect. She made an effort to look cheerful. 'Well . . . it's no use worrying about it now. We'll have to lift the potatoes by hand.'

Jimmy found a couple of forks, and armed with sacks they set out for the potato fields, the dog running ahead of them. The sun was beginning to warm through Maggie's anorak, and the land lay rich, refreshed by the recent rain, soft and springy beneath her feet, but she hardly noticed. Her mind was filled with the problem of her father. How long had he been like this? Now that she was home surely he would improve ... but just how bad had things become, and what other shocks did Ballybrae hold in store for her?

At the far side of the field they had to cross the stream, usually a mere trickle, but today swollen with rain and racing brown with mud, almost level with the log bridge Da had built so that he could drive the tractor over it into the next field.

'Mind how you go,' said Jimmy. 'The logs are slippy.'

Maggie kicked one of them. 'They're pretty rotten too.' She crossed carefully. That was one more thing she would have to talk to her father about. She stopped for a moment, and stared back across the fields to the little white-washed cottage, her face sombre. For all that she had been so eager to leave it, Ballybrae was her home. Life had been hard, but there had been happy times too. Her mother had been a strong woman, strong enough to provide backbone for the charming but weak man she had loved and married. And now her father had been left too long on his own. All the same, if Seamus Monohan had still been alive Da wouldn't be in this state.

She turned to Jimmy, who was patiently waiting for her. 'Have you met the new owner of the Big House?'

'Mr Blair? Oh yes, that I have.'

Maggie looked at him enquiringly. 'What d'you think of him?'

He shrugged. He obviously wondered what she was getting at. 'He's all right,' he said carelessly. 'Shall we be getting on?'

They started walking again, Maggie's mind filled with new thoughts. Adam Blair. So much depended on him . . . but what was he *really* like? Last night she had felt . . . well just what had it amounted to? she thought scornfully. A flicker of empathy between them . . . a strong attraction on her part. Was it possible to feel that, on such short acquaintance? But then, she reflected, how long had it taken for her to fall for Malcolm's charms? It only showed that her judgement in men was none too good.

Nevertheless, this man was far more disturbing and vital than Malcolm had ever been. It had only been a casual encounter, and yet he had captured her imagination completely — made it run riot — enough even to make her blush. Strange, when she didn't even know what he really looked like, she had been with him for such a short while and it had been dark. All that remained was the impression of a strong man — not just physically, but sure enough of himself to be interested in others . . . in her. A kind man, she had thought him. There you were. Wrong again!

'Here we are,' said Jimmy, breaking into her thoughts.

Maggie came back to reality. Long rows of potato plants lay waiting to be lifted and sorted. 'Let's get on with it,' she said.

A full hour's digging proved that the

land was in no fit state to work by hand. It was too wet. It clung to the forks in great sticky clods, heavy to lift, and the potatoes had to be clawed out with bare hands before they could be dropped into the sacks. Bent over, and growing hotter by the minute she worked doggedly beside Jimmy, digging and lifting and packing. After a while she removed her jacket, and rolled up her sleeves. The soil caked on her hands, forcing its way under her fingernails. Her hair worked free of its restraining band, and when she pushed away the dark strands she left filthy streaks across flushed cheeks. It was back-breaking . . . and even Maggie had to admit it eventually.

She groaned as she straightened up. 'It's no good.' She touched the boy on the shoulder. 'Stop, Jimmy. Thanks for trying, but it's hopeless. Perhaps it'll have dried out a bit by tomorrow.' She was glad to hear him heave a sigh of relief. She would have hated him to think her feeble.

'What shall I do then?' he asked.

A wave of helplessness swept over her. What could he do? What could anyone do? The whole place had been allowed to run down. What had been a thriving business was now no more than a liability.

'You'd better see what else we can collect for the market. I've got to go to the shops anyway. *Is* there more stuff to take?'

He brightened up. 'Sure . . . there's still veg. I'll do what I can. Hey — isn't that Mr Blair?'

She narrowed her eyes against the sun, looking across the field. Up the lane towards Ballybrae drove a cavalcade of vehicles, first a Land Rover, followed by her own car, and another one bringing up the rear. They stopped at the yard gate, and someone got out of the first vehicle. The air of authority was unmistakable — the set of the shoulders, broad and confident to a point just this side of arrogance. A wave of anticipation rose in her, but she beat it down. There was surely nothing to feel pleased about at the arrival of Adam Blair!

'Jimmy,' she said abruptly. 'Could you manage by yourself? I have to speak to that man . . . and the sooner the better.'

Slipping and sliding, her boots clumsy with the mud that had built up under them, she ran down the field, hoping that Adam Blair would not disappear before she'd had the chance of telling him just what she thought of him. But he had seen her. By the time she had recrossed the logs and reached Ballybrae the other vehicle had gone, but he was still there leaning against the gate, his arms folded over the top rail, as she arrived so out of breath that she had to cling to the wall, gasping.

He looked at her impassively, only the slightest twitch at the corners of his mouth showing that he found her amusing. 'Hello there. I saw you coming — you didn't need to gallop.' He opened the gate, and she stalked

45

through it, awkwardly conscious that her hair was flying in all directions, and her face no doubt crimson.

'I've brought back your car,' he added. 'No damage, you'll be pleased to hear.'

A quick glance was enough to take in every aspect of him, from the expensively-cut tweed jacket that fitted his broad shoulders so perfectly, to the shine on his shoes. No trampling through the mud for him! He looked even better than she remembered, heavily built but not running to fat; thick brown hair swept back at the temples; warm hazel eyes under those deceptively sleepy lids, and a mouth that was both firm and sensuous. Even his voice was pleasant . . . deep . . . cultured. She remembered that voice from her dream. Why, she thought with a pang, did he have to be quite so attractive?

'I'll take your word for it,' she said stiffly.

He raised his eyebrows. 'Do I detect

an air of disapproval?'

'Does it surprise you?'

His eyes travelled slowly from her tousled mane of hair and mud-streaked face, to the check shirt that strained at its buttons, hinting at the ripeness of the figure beneath. A half-smile hovered around his lips. 'I thought we got on pretty well, last night.'

She threw back her head, giving him look for look. 'That was before I had spoken with my father.'

His eyes returned to her face. 'Ah . . . Where is he?'

'He's in bed,' said Maggie bluntly. ' . . . drunk.'

The smile widened to a grin — and then a delighted chuckle. 'Maggie Nolan . . . you certainly have a way of saying things. Are you always so frank?'

Annoyance boiled up in her. 'It may seem very funny to you,' she retorted, 'but I don't see the joke in it. My Da is a good man. Seamus Monohan knew that. He would never have brought him to this state. How can you live with yourself, Mr Adam Blair?' She stopped, aghast. She must placate this man, not antagonize him. 'Perhaps you might not know it, being a stranger,' she continued more softly, 'but it has always been the practice to take small loans for seeds and fertilizers. Mr. Monohan never used to press for payment.' Despite her good intentions, scorn crept in, hardening the tactful phrases. 'He would never have threatened my Da with losing the tenancy . . . hounding him over a few miserable pounds . . . '

His smile had faded, his brows drawn together over eyes grown cold. 'And you think I've done that?'

'I know you have . . . ' She faltered, innate honesty causing her to add ' . . . my father told me so, and I believe him.'

He gave a short laugh. 'I'm a businessman, Miss Nolan. I have to protect my investments . . . '

'You needn't worry!' she flared. 'I'll repay every penny . . . '

She broke off, as he turned and strode purposefully towards his vehicle. 'Here!' she cried, leaping after him and catching hold of his sleeve. 'I haven't finished with you.'

He looked down, and she let go hastily. 'Nor I with you,' he said. 'Get in. We'll go to my office.'

He was right, she knew. This was not the place to continue the discussion. But on his premises he would have the upper hand.

'I must go into town. There's hardly any food in the house.'

'Suit yourself. But if you really want to help your father, we'll sort this out now.' A look of cynicism crossed his features. 'Or is it all talk? You haven't seemed that bothered about him.'

Maggie didn't hesitate any longer. She leapt up beside him, and slammed the door.

'Mind my hinges,' he said easily, as he let in the clutch.

'Damn your hinges! That was a foul thing to say.'

'It got you in here, didn't it?' Good humoured once more, he chuckled. 'What a little firebrand you are. I'm not really as bad as all that.' He could have been reading her mind.

She glared. 'I'm not a child. And I'm not all that little.'

That amused him too. 'Truthful as ever, Maggie. You're a fine strapping wench.'

That was worse! Enraged, she turned to speak, but she caught him looking at her, and stopped. The expression in his eyes was enigmatic. How was she to react to him? She had never met a man — not even Malcolm — whom she couldn't either manage or walk away from . . . but with this man she could do neither. She stole another sideways look and thankfully his eyes were now on the road. He had a well-moulded mouth with the lower lip a little full. It should have been a good-natured mouth, turning up at the corners, only that he kept it clamped together tightly, as if he was keeping strong appetites and strong emotions in check. But it was not a cruel mouth. Maggie felt sure it could make a woman happy . . . oh, damn that dream!

She wrenched her mind away from the wayward thoughts, and recalled his bitterness when they had spoken about women. Had someone hurt him? Tenderness welled up at the thought and she was consumed by the desire to put her arms around him . . . to pull his head down against her breast and comfort him, as she had comforted her father the night before. She pulled herself together, horrified. What on earth had got into her? Of all the men she had ever met, Adam Blair was the last to need her sympathy. If a woman had hurt him, he probably deserved it. She would do well to remember that. She clasped her fingers together in her lap, and was annoyed to find them trembling. It was all the fault of last night's dream. It had put ideas into her head that bore no resemblance to reality.

All the same, she could not help wondering what kind of women Adam Blair had known in the past. She could imagine them, smooth and confident with the gloss that money brought, knowing the score and never making the mistake of falling in love. Maggie sat up straight, and clenched her nails into her palms. She was beginning to be afraid that it would be all too easy to fall in love with Adam Blair.

For a while she sat in stunned silence, unnerved by her own thoughts. Everything was strangely changed, as though there had been a shift in reality; the distant shapes of the Kerry Hills sharper than ever before; the dry-stone walls edging the fields in a chequer-board pattern; the shadows of puffy white clouds racing like horses across the grass below. At last even the silence itself changed, becoming so revealing that she simply had to break it.

'Do you . . . ' her voice came out in a squeak, and she coughed to cover her embarrassment. 'Do you like living here — or will you be returning to England, Mr Blair?' It sounded stilted, even to her own ears.

'Adam.' He made it sound like an order. 'Unless you want me to call you Miss Nolan all the time.' That was softer, more friendly. His mind was on the steering and he had not noticed her awkwardness. She was pleased to feel the fluttering inside her subsiding.

'Adam, then. Looking after this estate must be difficult, if you are already in business in England.' That was better, let him see that she was as cool and collected as he had first believed her to be. She was so busy congratulating herself that she nearly missed what he was saying.

' . . . it fits in very well, as a matter of fact. I was looking for new outlets.' The road narrowed where it crossed the stream, and he paused to let a small boy on a bicycle ride past. ' . . . Now I'm ready to start up in Ireland. Encourage new industry . . . create new jobs.' He turned to her, smiling. 'I like to think

Uncle Seamus would have approved of Blairs of Devon expanding into Blairs of Duncow . . . '

'You are Blairs of Devon!' It hadn't occurred to her that he had anything to do with the vast commercial empire that dealt with so many aspects of the agricultural scene, from the production of foodstuffs, to chains of supermarkets. And yet, it followed. Hadn't she known he would be top of whatever sphere he had chosen? She had been right. There could be nobody more on top than the head of Blairs.

He looked surprised. 'Why — have you heard of us? I wouldn't have thought it much in your line.'

Talk about the long arm of coincidence! Malcolm's firm had dealt with all the market research for the network. She had joined them as a secretary, but had risen to the responsible position of personal assistant to Malcolm himself — and it had been purely on her merit, regardless of what some people might have thought. Oh yes . . . she knew quite a lot about Blairs of Devon!

'As a matter of fact . . . '

'Here we are,' Adam interrupted. 'I expect you'll find a few changes.'

Tall creations of intricate wrought-iron work between massive stone pillars, the gates of the Big House lay open before them. In his uncle's time they had always been firmly closed, underlining the difference in station between those who lived behind them, and the world outside. The drive too had been improved, and the wheels of the Land Rover crunched on the newly gravelled surface. Nearer the house the gloomy shrubbery had been cleared away, revealing the solid gothic lines of the large grey stone building. Flower beds still held the colour of autumn blooms.

'I take it you've been here before.'

She gave a slight smile. 'As a child — singing carols.' In those days she had hardly been in Seamus Monohan's social circle. Her father's friends tended to be a bit on the rough and ready side, fellow smallholders or mates from the racetrack, though Maggie's mother had come from more genteel stock. At the wide stone steps she hung back, looking down at her mud-encrusted boots. 'I hardly think . . .'

Adam smiled. 'You're right — I don't think Mrs Murphy would approve. Slip them off, and leave them here by the door.'

It wasn't really a question of slipping them off, they were a tight fit, with the thick socks she wore inside. Maggie wobbled on one leg as she eased off the second boot. He caught her around the waist, and pulled her back against him, sliding his hands around her body until they locked around her midriff, his mouth close to her ear, his breath tickling. Worse still, he had heard her quick intake of breath — she was sure he had — *and* noticed her telltale stiffening.

'My mother will be here soon,' he said casually. 'She likes to check that her dear son is still alive. So, let's get to business.'

'Fine by me!' she said sharply, pulling away from him. So, she was to be put in her place? Well, he needn't think she had wanted to be held like that. Crossly she dumped her boots and followed him.

The house too was very different. Someone had redecorated it — Adam himself, she supposed — if so, he had good taste. Gone was the heavily embossed wallpaper and dark paint-work. Now the walls were a cool jade green with carpets to match; just as well she *had* left her boots outside, she thought with a wry smile. Looking down, she noticed a large hole in the toe of one of her socks, and felt an absurd desire to hide it — but Adam Blair was not bothering to look at such things. He led her into the sitting room.

'Beautiful,' she sighed, enviously.

'You like it?' He looked pleased. 'A firm from Cork carried out the work, but I chose everything . . . I rather enjoyed it.'

And made a great job of it, Maggie thought appreciatively. The jade colour was extended here, with the same white woodwork. Inviting armchairs and a sofa faced an open stone fireplace in which a logfire was burning. Either side alcoves held shelves filled with books, and on the walls were several bright paintings, which she guessed were original Flamberts. At the far side of the room a large bow window, with a cushioned window seat, looked out onto a paved patio.

'It's the kind of house I've always dreamed of,' she admitted.

He looked at her thoughtfully, his head on one side, but made no comment, then he opened another door. 'We're talking business,' he reminded her.

Maggie flung her head up, and walked through stiff-backed. Inside though, she could not help but be intrigued. Here was an office with no expense spared to make it efficient and up-to-date. Filing cabinets lined the walls, with space for telex, typewriter, and two large desks. There was a computer with its monitor and printer, and on the walls were charts and graphs, but there was nothing personal in the room, not a photograph . . . not even a potted plant.

'No secretary yet.' He spoke casually, as if a secretary was merely another piece of electronic wizardry. 'I'll advertize.'

'I could work for you,' said Maggie.

He whirled around, and she was pleased to see the surprise on his face. It took something to shake this man.

'You?' He was looking at her as though she had sprouted horns.

'Why not?' A tremor of excitement crept up her spine, but she banished it as having no relevance. This was purely business, and a way out of both of their difficulties. 'I can assure you, I *am* qualified,' she said solemnly. 'And experienced.'

'What a surprising young woman you are, Maggie Nolan,' he murmured, a slight tremor that was suspiciously like laughter in his voice. 'Yes — I remember, you are very experienced!'

That would teach her to tell her life story to a complete stranger! She flushed, but studiedly ignored his innuendo.

'I'm a competent shorthand typist, and I can use audio equipment and the word processor,' she replied crisply. 'You could deduct my wages, to pay off the debt my father owes. It would solve both our problems, Mr Blair.'

'Adam,' he insisted.

'Adam, then.' She stood her ground, looking at him expectantly, half-smiling, willing him to accept her offer. At first he seemed to hesitate. Then he pulled forward a chair.

'Sit down, Maggie my dear,' he said gently.

He turned to one of the filing cabinets, and pulled out a folder. Taking it to the far side of the desk he sat down facing her, but he wasn't looking at her, he was staring down at the file in his broad capable hands. At last he opened it, and as he lifted his head she surprised a look of compassion.

'You're very loyal, Maggie,' he said, as if he found this a strange thing for anyone to be.

She felt uneasy. 'Why wouldn't I be? My father is a good man. Oh . . . I realize he's been foolish, but once I pay you back . . . '

'Maggie . . . ' He turned the file, almost as if it was distasteful to him, and pushed it towards her. 'This is what your father owes.'

She bent forward to scan the figures, and felt the blood draining from her face as she gripped the edge of the desk. 'I . . . I don't understand. But this is for thousands.' Her eyes searched his anxiously. 'Da can't have borrowed all this. What could he possibly have needed it for?'

He shrugged. 'Judging from the receipts and the entries in the ledger, the loans were for new equipment to modernize your father's market garden.'

Maggie shook her head. 'But . . . there hadn't been anything new,' she said huskily. 'Even the tractor's had it. That's the trouble, we're out of date and unproductive. We need equipment, but we haven't had any . . . I can swear to that.'

He leaned back in his chair, and smiled a little wearily. 'There's more than tractors and cultivators in Duncow, Maggie.'

For a moment she didn't understand him . . . and then the painful truth dawned. 'Oh no . . . not *the races*!' She could hear an echo from the past, her mother's angry voice. 'If you don't keep from the betting, Bonnie Nolan, I'll leave you . . . you can depend on that.'

'My uncle was very fond of your father,' Adam continued, his deep voice breaking into her thoughts, 'so I tried to stop him. Then I suggested retirement. I could have given him a smaller cottage, and let somebody else work the land. You do see . . . '

'Yes . . . ' she cut in hastily. 'I . . . I understand. I'm sorry . . . ' She stood to go, sick with shame and disgust, wanting to escape the pity in his eyes. She had been so ludicrously naïve, offering her services. What good would that do — a mere drop in the ocean? No wonder he laughed at her. 'I apologize for taking up your time.'

He stopped her before she reached the door. 'Look at me, Maggie.' He laid his hands on her shoulders. She could feel their warmth through her shirt, and something lurched inside. She closed her eyes. Hadn't she enough on her mind, without the treacherous response of her own body to contend with? Whatever she had felt, whatever she had imagined *he* might feel too, it was all over now. She was only an embarrassing red line in his ledger.

'Look at me,' he repeated.

She did not dare lift her gaze any higher than his chin. Even that was disturbing. It was a good chin, firm and clean cut . . .

'Straight in the eyes . . . I won't have less.'

His voice was insistent. He was a man used to giving orders, and Maggie found herself instinctively obeying, stripped of all her pride, baring to him the pain that was evident in her great grey eyes.

He touched her mud-stained cheek, running his fingers along the fine line of her jaw, turning his wrist to cup her chin in his hand. 'Your father's gambling isn't your fault,' he said gently. 'It'll have to stop, but if the offer still stands, there's a job here for you.' He tilted her face up to his, and leaning forward, kissed her. His lips were warm and gentle against hers. It was the kind of kiss you would give a child that had been hurt.

She clenched her fists, keeping her arms stiff by her sides. It wasn't his fault that her pulse leaped, wanting it to be so much more, that her lips were ready to part beneath his, urging her to cling, that a flame was melting something at her core. Her hands almost reached out to draw him closer — almost — but she had just enough strength to fight the impulse. His only purpose had been to comfort her, she recognized that.

She drew back from him. 'You really mean it?'

His eyelids drooped, and his lips went back to their usually clamped expression. 'I said so,' he answered curtly.

She took a deep breath. 'Then I'll start tomorrow. What I said about taking my wages still stands. It . . . it's all I can think of for the moment, but I'll pay you back somehow, I promise.'

He nodded. Was that gleam in his hazel eyes satisfaction? No doubt he was glad to be getting something back out of all this. If only Seamus Monohan had not let her father have so much money — but then he had been getting old, and had probably not realized how the debt was building up.

'Good!' He returned her father's file to the cabinet, business-like again. 'Now — your shopping. And stop worrying.'

Maggie was about to thank him once more, when a horn sounded. She looked out of the window in time to see a car draw up, and a smart grey-haired woman — obviously his mother — step out. It was easy to see the resemblance to Adam in the strong features and the confident bearing, but what showed as strength in him seemed somewhat daunting in her. After her came an exquisitely petite woman in a silver fur coat. She had a small face with delicate features and huge eyes framed by short stylishly-cut blonde hair. Maggie had imagined the kind of woman Adam was used to, now here was the reality. The visitor tucked her arm through Mrs Blair's in a gesture of familiarity. She must be someone Adam knew well. Maggie found the thought depressing.

'My God!'

She turned in surprise. Adam's face was white, his nostrils pinched. She reached out her hand.

'Are you all right?'

He looked at her blankly for a second, as if in shock. Then his expression changed to one of disgust. His eyes darkened. His mouth thinned into a bitter line. For a moment he had been shaken . . . appeared at a loss . . . but it had not lasted. Now, decisive as ever, he wheeled towards her.

'Will you do something for me?'

At that moment she would have done anything to stop him from looking so tortured. 'But what . . . ?'

'There isn't time to explain. They'll be here any moment. Promise you'll back me up in anything I say or do in the next few minutes.' Then, as she stared back at him uncomprehendingly, 'I'll write off your father's debt . . . '

'Of course!' There was no need for him to promise anything. Whatever he wanted of her, she was willing to give . . . she already knew that. Then the door opened.

'Adam, darling.' The grey-haired woman swept in. She gave Maggie one brief incurious glance, before kissing her son. 'We've had a horrible journey . . . and all for your sake.'

'We, mother?' He was holding himself in check. Maggie could feel the tension in him, like a coiled spring ready to break at any moment.

'Yes dear. I met Irene. Now, I *know* you'll be cross with me, but poor dear, she needed peace and quiet . . . and who better to understand her than you? I *insisted* that she come with me.'

On cue, the other woman arrived. She made an elegant picture, framed in the doorway. Maggie felt that she knew it too — and then chided herself for being critical. The newcomer turned her great eyes on Adam, and slowly stretched out her arms.

'Forgive me, but I just had to come.' Her voice was attractively husky. 'I knew you'd understand. Darling — it's wonderful to see you again.' Floating past Maggie as though she was not there, she stood on tiptoe in front of Adam, and curled her arms around his neck.

As if she owned him! thought Maggie. She wished she was anywhere but in this room, witnessing this. She steeled herself for the sight of Adam bending to kiss the upturned mouth . . . but instead he gently removed the arms that entwined him, and turned in her direction.

'Maggie . . . may I introduce my mother, and Mrs Manson.' His face was inscrutable as he took the two short steps that brought him to Maggie's side. He put his arm around her waist, and his fingers tightened convulsively against her.

'Mother . . . Irene . . . may I introduce Miss Maggie Nolan . . . my fiancée!'

3

'*Adam!*'

Maggie wasn't sure which of them gasped his name. It might well have been herself. Irene Manson's face blanched, her lipstick standing out a red gash against its pallor. Her eyes devoured Adam, and he stared back at her.

It was Mrs Blair who broke the spell. 'Well, I must say, you do spring some surprises on us. Come here child.'

Maggie stepped forward in a daze. When he had asked for help she had never expected this. What on earth was he thinking of? Resentful, she stood while his mother's critical glance took in the mud-stained clothes right down to the socks and the all too obvious hole. Mrs Blair didn't miss a thing, and her powdered face with its pencil-thin eyebrows showed clearly what she thought.

Maggie looked in appeal at Adam's enigmatic face. How dare he put her in this position . . . was it his idea of a joke? No . . . he was on edge, a muscle twitching in his jaw. Whatever else it was, there was nothing funny about it. He had asked for her help, and she had promised. All right — if he wanted her to play his game, so be it. She didn't know his reasons, but she felt the urgency of his need — and that was enough.

'How d'you do, Mrs Blair. Adam has told me so much about you.' That was a lie, for starters, but her voice was steady, with just the right amount of warmth mingled with shyness. She held out her hand. Adam's mother gazed at it in horror. Maggie looked at it herself — a filthy paw, even now dropping flakes of dried mud on the expensive carpet. She flushed, and put it behind her back. 'Perhaps not!' she said brightly. 'I've been lifting potatoes,' she added.

Adam came to her rescue. 'Maggie's father farms part of the estate.'

'Indeed?' Mrs Blair did not look impressed. 'And how long have you known one another?'

'Not long . . . '

'Ages . . . '

'Though it doesn't seem long, does it darling?' added Adam.

'No — no time at all!' agreed Maggie. Any more of this and she would not be able to hold back the nervous giggle rising in her throat; if he imagined he could carry this off, he was crazy. Mrs Blair was not the sort of woman to be easily fooled.

'Maggie's agreed to help me with the business,' continued Adam. He seemed more relaxed now, addressing himself directly to his mother. 'It'll be a great asset, to have her interested, and, naturally, it will be pleasant to be able to work together. We . . . '

'Oh . . . ' It was only a little gasp, but enough to make them turn around.

Irene Manson swayed, a hand to her forehead. Then, before their eyes, she crumpled into a heap on the floor. With muttered words too low to be heard, Adam sprang to her side.

'Help me get her onto the sofa.'

He slid his arm under her shoulders, and Maggie took her legs. She weighed no more than a child, exotic perfume wafting from the enveloping furs. Maggie noticed the sheer nylons, the delicate ankles, high-arched feet in expensive shoes. Her gaze travelled to the pale features, so perfect and delicate. Adam's expression told her nothing, but she could feel waves of strong emotion emanating from him. It made her feel strangely cold inside — who was this woman who had such a profound effect on him?

Mrs Blair had been hovering anxiously. 'I told you, she's had a hard time. She's still terribly upset over Charles's death . . . poor dear. Shouldn't you send for a doctor?'

'No,' said Adam bleakly. 'I doubt if

there's much wrong.'

Mrs Blair gave a snort of exasperation. Who could blame her? thought
Maggie, looking at those eyelashes lying
dark on Mrs Manson's cheeks. How
could Adam be so callous?

The eyelashes fluttered, almost as
though they were too thick and heavy to
be raised. Irene moved, and then sank
back wearily.

'Don't get up yet,' urged Maggie,
restraining her. 'You fainted. Do you
feel better now?' She noticed that
Irene's eyes, now open, were pale green
and cool, slanting at the corners, like a
cat's.

She favoured Maggie with a look,
and the eyes narrowed. 'How sweet!'
Then her glance dismissed Maggie, and
she put out a slender hand to Adam.
'Perhaps I should not have come.' The
red lips quivered pathetically. 'But life
has been so difficult for me recently
— you've no idea. I didn't know where
to turn, and then I thought . . . of you.'
She began caressing Adam's sleeve.

He detached himself, and crossing the room flung himself into one of the low armchairs. He sat hunched in it, with his long legs sprawled out, his eyes mere slits.

'Very kind of you,' he drawled. 'But I don't see how I can help.'

Her eyes widened, and she pouted coyly. 'I'm sure you *do*, darling,' she purred. 'Especially since I have something you want . . . which I may be willing to let you have . . . at the right price!'

She turned then to Maggie. 'My dear! You must please tell me if I'm in the way. Adam is very naughty not to have told us of his engagement — but he always was impulsive. A long, long time ago . . . ' her voice sank confidentially, ' . . . Adam and I were *very* close.'

She could hardly have spelled it out more clearly, thought Maggie — and a fat lot of help Adam was, standing there as if turned to stone, a mocking smile tugging at the corners of his mouth. What on earth was she supposed to say to all this? It wouldn't be so bad if she had the remotest idea of what it was all about. Something was going on, that much was clear. She managed a smile.

'Of course you aren't in the way. Any friend of Adam must be welcome here.' She gave a little laugh. 'There's enough room.'

'And are you staying here, Miss Nolan?' It was his mother, thinking the worst, Maggie had no doubt.

'No,' she answered calmly. 'I have a home of my own to go to, and a father to look after.'

Suddenly she felt she'd had enough. 'I don't want to appear rude, but if everything is all right now, I really should get back.' Anything — *anything* to escape!

Adam jumped to his feet. 'And I promised to take you shopping.' The teasing look he turned on her held all the intimacy of a lover. It hit her with a shock. What an actor . . . and how hard to remember that he *was* only acting. It would be so easy to slide under the spell of the fantasy . . . but that's all it was, more's the pity. Maggie allowed herself a brief moment's indulgence of imagining how she would feel if it had been real — if she had *really* been the woman in Adam Blair's life.

'Pop along and get your boots on, darling, and I'll be right with you,' he continued smoothly.

'Oh no!' said Maggie, jerked back to reality. She didn't want him with her, not in these circumstances, at any rate. All she wanted was to leave this intensely embarrassing situation, and to get back to normal where she could think straight. She needed to; ever since she had awoken from that dream this morning the day had progressed from bad to worse. 'I can find my own way back.'

With a word of farewell she left them, closing the door behind her. She had the feeling that Mrs Blair could hardly wait to see the back of her, and as for Irene Manson, if she was not mistaken that lady would be very glad to get

Adam to herself.

'Adam . . . what on earth are you playing at?'

The ringing tones were his mother's. They penetrated the door all too easily, and Maggie hesitated — not wanting to eavesdrop, but unable to tear herself away.

'You've done some stupid things in your time, but this really is the limit. Who is this great muddy girl? Why haven't you said anything about her before? You can't honestly expect me to believe there's anything in this engagement of yours . . . is she in trouble?'

The old vixen! The heat rising in her cheeks, her fists clenched indignantly — as though wanting nothing better than to thump her one — Maggie strained to hear just what Adam had to say in reply to his mother's accusations.

'Why . . . Maggie Nolan, as I live and breathe.'

'Oh!' Maggie whirled around guiltily, her face going even redder as she faced an aproned woman who had appeared as if from nowhere. 'Oh, Mrs Murphy, you startled me. I was just leaving.'

'Without saying a word to me. And after all those mincepies you used to gobble. Sure and that's a fine thing.'

The housekeeper was a cheerful angular soul, full of exclamations and memories of the days when Maggie had been but a scraggy youngster. 'Do you remember . . . ' all her sentences began. Maggie was forced to remain, on edge in case the door opened and they found her still there. She wanted to be gone . . .

'And how's Bonnie? I hear he's been . . . not too well?'

Mrs Murphy's face was shrewd but sympathetic. No doubt the whole neighbourhood knew of her father's foolishness. Was there no end to the embarrassment in this house?

'He's — well, he's not been so good. But now I'm home I'll have him right in no time.'

'I'm sure you will. I'm sure you will!'

'Well . . . ' She cast another agonized

glance at the door. 'I must go now, Mrs Murphy. It's been lovely seeing you again.'

'Give my regards to your father.'

'Oh yes . . . I shall.' She was out of the front door like a shot. And what would Mrs Murphy think when she heard about this sudden 'engagement'? she wondered helplessly, as she reclaimed her boots. What would everybody think? Well, Adam Blair had got them into this . . . let him do the explaining. At last she was ready, and with a sigh of relief set off to walk briskly back to Ballybrae. It was a fair step, but it would do her good. Then she heard running footsteps on the gravel behind her. She knew all too well who it would be.

'And where d'you think you're going?'

She turned. 'Why did you follow me? I'm going home.'

'Not on your own, you're not. We'll take the car.' This was the Adam Blair her father had told her about — the man who got what he wanted, and did not hesitate to ride roughshod over others to get it. She stood her ground.

'I don't *want* to go with you. Leave me alone.'

He was smiling as he came up to her, but his eyes were cold and the words that followed gritted between his teeth. 'You're my fiancée . . . remember? That was the bargain. Well — act like one.'

He kept the pretence up, all the way to the car, keeping his arm around her and bending his face towards her as though they were talking intimately. In case one of his visitors might be watching, she thought angrily . . . but which one did he most want to fool? Watch it! She could already feel a languorous warmth spreading through her limbs, simply because he was holding her. Why . . . oh why . . . did this man have such a violent effect on her? Nothing she had ever known before had prepared her for it, certainly not Malcolm.

At the car he stopped, and stood with

his hands spanning her waist as though measuring it, his hazel eyes examining her face . . . softening. 'I'm sorry, Maggie,' he said, apology in his voice. 'I shouldn't take it out on you.' Roughly he pulled her towards him, and held her in a bear-like embrace, his face buried in her hair.

She closed her eyes, and held her breath, feeling his breathing, his arms tight about her as she relaxed against him. Then, before she had a chance to respond, he released her with a sigh. He smelled of wood smoke, she thought shakily. Wood smoke and old tweed. She liked it, and she liked being held by him. It had felt warm, and protected, and good. She could put up with a lot of that. But then she saw a curtain move at one of the windows, and the feeling evaporated. The hug had obviously only been for the watcher's benefit.

It made her angry with herself, to find her senses betraying her in such a manner, with a man who was using her for his own ends. But then, she admitted, she was using him too, wasn't she . . . to save her father? They were no better than each other — but at least he knew her reasons, while she did not understand his at all.

Once they were on their way back to Ballybrae she echoed his mother's words. 'Adam . . . what *do* you think you're playing at?'

'Playing at? I'm going shopping with you, after you've cleaned up.' He looked inordinately pleased with himself, as if he had scored over someone — pulled off a business deal. Perhaps he had.

Maggie's lips tightened, and her eyes sparked dangerously. 'If you don't stop this car immediately . . . so help me, I'll . . . '

He brought it to a slithering halt in a field gateway. Turning, he slid an arm across the back of her seat. His other hand rose to touch her face, a quizzical smile lifting his mouth.

'What a fiery thing you are!' he murmured, his eyes fixed on the soft curve of her lips. 'And what would you have done if I hadn't stopped? Jumped out?' He began to rub his thumb gently across her lower lip. Maggie sat as though hypnotized, wanting to turn away, but unable to. Her mouth began to tingle, as though his touch was awakening it to throbbing life.

'Calm and collected I said, didn't I?' he mused. 'I should have known better, from the look of that mouth.' He bent his head towards her. 'Maggie . . . '

His eyes, she noticed vaguely, held little flecks of brown that made them warm and reassuring, small crinkles appearing at their corners when he smiled. His fingers spread out, sliding under her tangled hair to massage the nape of her neck, warm against her skin, sending delicious shivers down her spine, urging her own head forward slowly . . . and she knew then that — more than anything in the world — she wanted him to kiss her.

With a jerk she placed both hands against his chest, and held him off, forcing herself to sound cold, antagonistic. 'Don't you think you should explain this play-acting?'

He returned her forthright stare. One eyebrow lifted but after a moment he shrugged and withdrew his arm.

'Let's put it this way. I wipe out your father's debt. You play my fiancée. It should only be for a few days, until Irene gets bored and decides to leave.' He was quite matter of fact. He could have been discussing one of his many business deals. That's all it was really; a business deal she could not afford to refuse.

'I understand that perfectly well,' she snapped back at him. 'But what I want to know is . . . *why?*'

He gave a muttered curse. 'Was there ever such a woman for putting things straight?'

'You'll be glad of that,' she asserted. 'When I start work.'

'Humph!' His brows drew together in a frown. For some reason he looked quite put out. 'Have you heard of

Manson's Transport?'

'Of course,' said Maggie. 'You can hardly miss them . . . all those big white lorries with the red lettering on them.'

'Exactly. And you'll remember I mentioned a takeover bid? Well, I've been negotiating for some time to acquire enough shares to take them over. I need them — particularly now.'

She was beginning to understand. 'And Irene Manson . . . ?'

'Has a controlling vote. She's obviously tumbled to who is buying up the shares. That's why she's here.'

Maggie's forehead creased. 'But I don't understand. Mrs Manson said she was willing to give you what you wanted.'

He kept his eyes on a lock of her hair, twining it around his fingers, as if fascinated by it. Maggie fought to keep her mind on what he was saying, though the light, gentle pull of his fingers on her hair carried a charge right back to its roots. All the feelings of her body seemed to concentrate on that one, tiny section of her scalp, and then to pour back over her in numbing waves of languor.

'At a price,' he murmured. 'That's why I need you, Maggie.'

'As a bodyguard!' She could not help smiling. The idea was ridiculous, she had never known anyone more capable of looking after himself. 'Against . . . the tiny Mrs Manson?'

He looked up. 'Don't be fooled by Irene. She isn't as soft and helpless as she looks.'

Maggie felt strangely perverse. 'I thought she was sweet.'

'That's what she wants you to feel. A great one for working on people's emotions, our Irene.'

He started up the engine, as though the matter, for him, was finished — but he still hadn't really answered her question. She was no nearer understanding why Irene Manson disturbed him so, or what her relationship with him had been.

Maggie had never been one for

beating about the bush; if she wanted to know something she found the best way was to ask. 'What harm could that woman *possibly* have done you, that you should be so nasty to her? Why do you need me as a shield between you both . . . and such an expensive shield at that?'

'There you go again — wanting to know everything,' he murmured. 'Let it be, Maggie. It's a long story.'

'Going back to a long, long time ago,' she mocked, echoing Irene's words. She longed to shake him, to force the truth out of him, even if it was something she didn't really want to hear.

'But why is she here? She does seem to be in some sort of trouble. Perhaps she does need help. Don't you think . . . '

'No I don't.' He changed gear viciously. 'Kindly let me be the judge of Irene's intentions.'

Maggie was startled by the stark anger in his voice. 'I'm sorry . . . I only thought . . . '

'Well don't! Just do as I ask.'

Maggie sat rigid, her face flushed. He glanced at her, and his tone softened. 'Please, Maggie.'

'I . . . oh, very well. If it'll help.'

'It will. Believe me.'

As they continued in silence back to Ballybrae Maggie tried to make sense of what had happened. She could understand his business reasons for wanting Mrs Manson's shares, and that Irene was using her knowledge of this for her own purposes. The memory of Irene's thin pale fingers caressing Adam's sleeve came into Maggie's mind. Yes . . . she could well imagine what Mrs Manson might want. But was his business so important to Adam that he would conjure up a bogus fiancée, just to keep Irene at bay, without offending her? It seemed it was. She had heard of men who put business before everything else. Adam, it appeared, was one of them.

She sighed, thinking how complicated life had become. Still, one thing was clear . . . he *was* going to help her father, and that was what she had to remember. That was why she was falling in with this deception. Her father would be able to keep his home, and she would have a job . . . and she would be with Adam. But of course that had nothing to do with it. That *certainly* was not the reason she was going along with his crazy scheme . . .

When they stopped in Ballybrae yard, Adam gathered up her hands and held them in his own, close to his body.

'Happier now?'

She was afraid to look up. 'Yes . . . no . . . I don't know!'

He stroked her hair, and the fire leapt inside her again. She felt its heat at the nape of her neck, then in her spine. She shook him off with an angry toss of her head, but his eyes remained gentle and understanding.

'Poor Maggie,' he murmured soothingly. 'Still pining for . . . Matthew, was it?'

'Malcolm,' she corrected, still not

90

meeting his eyes, 'but . . . '

'I know you'd rather be with him. But trust me — and at least pretend to be in love. It's only for a few days, and it'll get your father out of his mess.'

Rather be with Malcolm! Whatever gave him that idea? She hadn't really loved Malcolm, she knew that now. She had simply been flattered that he had noticed her, a girl fresh from the country. She opened her mouth to say so, but stopped. Better that Adam should go on believing she loved Malcolm. It would be too embarrassing if he guessed her dawning feelings for *him*. He might even withdraw his offer of a job. No . . . it would not do if he found out — it would not do at all!

She shrugged. 'Why not?' she said lightly. 'I think you're crazy, but you've been so kind about Da, I can hardly say no.'

He let go of her hands. He didn't look all that grateful. In fact he frowned, his brows meeting in a straight line as though something she had said displeased him, but all he said was 'Good — I'm glad we're agreed on that, at least.'

'There's one thing I'm puzzled about, though,' said Maggie. 'I mean . . . I imagine you've had lots of women friends.'

He smiled, those crinkles at the corners of his eyes deepening. 'Forthright as ever, Maggie. What are you getting at?'

She pursed her lips, looking at him, her head on one side. 'Why is your mother so keen on Irene?' she asked bluntly. 'I can see why you find her attractive, but why is your mother pushing her?'

'Don't you know?' He looked at her with bewilderment that faded as he made some new connection in his mind. 'No . . . of course you wouldn't. Irene is my wife.'

Maggie's stomach took a lurch. No wonder Irene had signalled 'hands off'. His wife! Why . . . the beast . . . he was no better than Malcolm. She began to scramble out of the car. Adam leaped out on his side and caught hold of her by her jacket. She wheeled around, and tried to knock his arm away, but her punch might as well have been aimed at an oak tree. With a jerk he pulled her to him, wrapping his arms around her to smother her attack.

'Let me go!' she stormed. 'How dare you trick me into something like this, *using* me, when all the time . . . '

'Whoa there. Calm down.' He might have been gentling an unbroken horse, stroking her neck, laying his cheek against hers. She stood stiff and unyielding in his embrace, though the desire was leaping through her again, urging her to melt into his warmth, to show him her true feelings, and be damned to other people. But it was no use feeling like that. Other people existed, and one of them was Adam's wife. He'd better have a good explanation for this one!

He had. 'My ex-wife, I should have

said. I forgot you had a thing about marriage.'

Maggie slowly relaxed. She pushed him away so that she could look into his face. Of course he was telling the truth — he wouldn't be looking so amused otherwise. She seemed to be providing a neverending source of entertainment for him, she thought crossly. Would she ever learn not to react so quickly?

'Charles Manson — Irene's husband — was my partner once. I wasn't so successful in those days, and Charles had more money. It looked as though he would make the big time first.' His lips twisted in a cynical smile. 'Irene and I were divorced. I'm a free man, Maggie. You're not wrecking a home.'

'And Charles has died?' She had to be sure she had it straight. 'And you want me because you think she might want you back?'

He hesitated, his eyebrows raised. 'As usual, you put things very clearly, my dear. That's one reason, yes.'

And the other was that he was short

of a secretary. What other reason could there be? She had no illusions about herself. She had no great claim to beauty — too tall for a start. 'Well built' her mother had described it tactfully. 'A great muddy girl,' Mrs Blair had called her with less sensitivity. So very different from Irene.

Maggie ran fingers through her hair. 'Adam! This whole thing is getting too complicated and ridiculous. We'd never carry it off.'

His arms tightened around her again, those warm brown-flecked eyes with their seductively heavy lids gazed into her. 'Please Maggie . . . ' he murmured. 'Please?'

He didn't need to plead with her, she thought despairingly. If he pressed for the money Da owed they would be ruined, and what could Da do at his age? It would kill him. If Adam wanted to he could simply command that she stick to her bargain . . . but he hadn't done that. He'd paid her the courtesy of making it sound as if she was doing him a favour.

'Oh very well,' she said helplessly. 'I don't have much choice, do I? But what am I to tell Da? He thinks you are the Devil incarnate. I'm inclined to agree with him.'

He laughed, perhaps glad too that the seriousness of the occasion had been broken. 'Are you now?' he chuckled, mocking the lilt of Irish in her voice. 'Then I'll have to see how I can change your mind.' He gave her a hefty smack on the bottom. 'Get into the house, woman, and get cleaned up. Leave your father to me.'

Inside they found Bonnie Nolan sitting in his chair by the fire, distinctly the worse for wear. He glanced up, his eyes flickering uneasily over Maggie's shoulder at the man following her.

'Ah, there you are Maggie,' he exclaimed querulously. 'I could have told you it was too wet for lifting 'taties. Wasn't that why I didn't bother getting up. I'll let Maggie lie in, I thought . . . '

Maggie wrapped her arms around

him. 'Da — didn't I tell you everything would be all right? I'm going up to wash, and Adam here has something to explain to you.'

'Maggie . . .' It was the cry of a child who sees his mother walk away, but Maggie steeled her heart and left the room, taking the steep stairs two at a time. She couldn't begin to guess what Adam would say to her father, or how Da would take it It might, thought Maggie as she washed away the remaining vestiges of mud, be easier not to explain too much. Da would get flaming angry if he thought she was being bought to pay for his debts.

Clean at last, she examined the contents of her suitcases for something suitable to wear, trying at the same time to ignore the hum of voices from downstairs. She hadn't even unpacked properly yet, and most of her clothes needed pressing. At last she found something fit to be seen in — a flowing brown woollen skirt that suited her height, and a soft sweater of russet and green mohair. As she pulled it over her head and arranged its cowl neckline, she scowled at herself in the mirror. She'd never been vain. On the other hand she hadn't been dissatisfied with her appearance either — not until now. But now, suddenly, everything had changed. Nothing seemed the same any more . . .

4

'Maggie . . . are you takin' all day up
there? Your poor man's waiting here
for you . . . and haven't I a word or two
to say myself, keeping me in the
dark like this, and you engaged all the
time.'

Her father didn't sound angry — that
was something, at least! In fact, he
sounded delighted. One never knew
how Da would take things. Like a child
he was, really.

'I'm coming, Da.'

One quick glance in the mirror, while
she swept her thick black hair into its
customary knot, and a quick dab of
powder, and a brush of colour on her
lips. She pulled a rueful face. Why
couldn't she have been born petite and
breathtakingly beautiful . . . but then, it
was no use comparing herself with
Irene Manson. Any woman would feel

inadequate beside her, let alone a great lump like herself. In any case, it was not her beauty Adam Blair wanted her for. Zipping up her suede boots, and snatching a thick green crocheted shawl, she made her way down the stairs.

'Ah, there you are.' Her father pounced on her, holding her at arm's length, admiringly. 'And don't you look a picture?' He turned to Adam Blair, who was leaning against the mantel of the fireplace, a glass in his hand, looking quite at ease. 'Doesn't she look a picture, Sorr?'

'Oh, indeed she does.' Adam's unfathomable eyes held hers mockingly. 'You look beautiful, darling.' Moving towards her he bent his head, and kissed her lingeringly on the mouth. There was nothing comforting about his kiss this time. He was being provoking, his lips moving on hers deliberately, firmly, as if to prove to himself — or to her — that she knew how to play her part. To show she did, she slid her arms up around his neck, and kissed him back without reservation. Immediately she felt a response leap in him. It excited and startled her. When she drew away she was still looking at him, wide eyed.

'Why didn't you tell me?' insisted her father.

She came to with a jerk. 'Er . . . tell you what, Da?'

'Why, would you listen to her! Tell me what, indeed. Tell me that you had met, back in London. Tell me that you were engaged, instead of letting me . . . well, I didn't understand, and perhaps I said things . . . ' He was getting uncomfortable, floundering.

Adam came to his aid. 'It was my fault. I made her keep it a secret until we could tell you together. Didn't I, my sweet?'

'Oh . . . yes.'

'And I needed her here, Mr Nolan, to explain to you about the help I hope to give you. If you'll be so gracious as to accept. I hope you won't mind my loaning you some men and equipment — for you to supervise, of course.'

Bonnie's face creased into a wide smile. He was fair hopping with excitement. 'Did you hear that, Maggie?' He hugged her again. 'Oh, your mother would be proud of you this day.'

Would she, indeed? Maggie doubted it. Her mother had hated lies . . . and this was the biggest lie of all. But what could she do? Was it too late to explain? She opened her lips to speak . . .

'Da . . .'

Adam broke in quickly. 'Maggie, we must get off to town now. I'd like to take you to lunch while we're there.'

Diverted, Maggie gasped. 'Goodness, is it that time already? But Da, you've not had anything to eat yet, I'll have to get you . . .'

'Ah no, no.' Her father held up a hand to stop her. 'I won't be needing anything Maggie, I've far too much to do. There's people to see, folks to tell.'

He clapped Adam on the shoulder. 'We'll have a ceilidh at the local, that's for sure.'

'It's a sort of a do . . . music, and dancing, and no doubt plenty of drinking,' explained Maggie distractedly, 'but Da . . . '

'That sounds interesting,' said Adam, 'and I'll look forward to it. But tonight I hope you'll dine with us. I want you to meet my mother.'

'Did you hear that?' Bonnie swelled visibly. 'Me eating at the Big House!'

'In that case I'll have to see you've a clean shirt, and press your suit — so we'd better be off now,' said Maggie drily. The thought of Mrs Blair's reaction to her father did not inspire her with any great delight. She turned in the doorway. 'Now see you're here when I get back, Da.' She ran back and whispered fiercely in his ear. 'And don't go drinking any more!'

★ ★ ★

Adam in a supermarket was like a child let loose in a toy shop, Maggie thought indulgently, as she watched him pushing a trolley before him with more energy than skill. Just as she thought she knew this man she discovered a new facet of his character.

'How d'you steer these things?' he complained ruefully. 'The wheels point the wrong way.'

Maggie laughed as she added eggs and sausages to her pile of provisions. 'Have you never been in a supermarket before?'

'Of course I have.' He gave her an offended look. 'I own a chain of the damned things.'

'Ah, but that's different! Shopping is a skill you have to learn. Look out!' She stopped him from running into a great pile of tinned beans. 'Anyway — it was your idea, to come along.'

'Am I complaining?' He stopped abruptly, to fling out his arms, blocking the aisle to the annoyance of the shoppers behind him. 'You wished to shop . . . and your wish is my command.'

'Adam!' Maggie laughed as she pushed him out of the way. She had to admit that he had been good company, light-hearted and amusing — something she had not expected from him — and it made it all the harder to remember that it was a sham. Who would have thought he was play-acting, seeing him so enthusiastically examining goods, checking prices, comparing contents. They would have been there all day, if she had not reminded him that it was lunchtime.

'I know just the place,' he said, 'but first there's something else we have to do.'

'What is it, Adam?' Maggie asked with interest when, the groceries packed away in the boot of the car, they set out on foot along the narrow pavements of Duncow High Street. Adam strode out on those long legs of his with such determination that she almost had to run by his side. 'Have

105

you some business to attend to in town? Will you slow down, please . . . you walk far too fast for me?'

He slowed down a little, and took her arm. 'Come along, Maggie . . . a big girl like you should be able to step out. Never mind, we're here now.' They had stopped outside a jewellers. 'We've got to buy the ring.'

'The ring!' She drew away from him.

'What's the matter now?' The look he turned on her was back to his old brooding self. 'You've got to have an engagement ring.'

'I don't see why,' Maggie objected. 'It seems so silly to buy a ring for such a short while. It isn't necessary. Lots of couples get engaged without having a ring these days.'

'Well I don't.' He bent down to peer into the shop window, absorbed in his scrutiny. 'Why do you object to wearing my ring?' he said icily. 'Is it so distasteful to you?'

'It isn't that . . . '

He stood erect again, and took her

arm to propel her smartly towards the shop door. 'Well, what then?' he demanded. 'Is it because I'm not Matthew?'

'Malcolm . . . ' He knew the name perfectly well, damn him. Her relaxed mood dissipated, she stiffened up against him. If he wanted the whole world to see him dragging her into the shop . . . so be it!

'Whatever his name is. Is that it?'

'No, of course not. It's just the expense . . . '

'Let me worry about that. It's my side of the bargain. You just concentrate on fulfilling your side, will you? Mother will expect to see a ring on your finger tonight.'

'And so will Mrs Manson.' She didn't know what made her add that. He dropped his hand from her arm.

'Yes,' he said coldly. 'So will Irene. If you're worrying about the cost — don't. I can always pawn it, when all this is over.'

She felt angry and heart-sore as she

followed him into the shop. It was so hard to walk the tightrope between reality and fantasy. The way he looked at her sometimes, she could be forgiven for thinking he more than liked her. His eyes, in the supermarket just now, there had been a warmth in them that surely was not faked, but it had faded the moment she mentioned his ex-wife. She lifted her head proudly, colour touching her high cheekbones. It was a good thing she had spoken Irene's name. It served to remind her how things really were . . .

'Which one do you fancy, darling?'

The manager brought out several trays of rings for Maggie to choose from. Reluctantly she tried on one after another. They were all beautiful, but it didn't seem right to be doing this. Of course, if it had been for real . . . well, that would have been different. But it wasn't real, and that was where the pain lay. Perhaps she should teach him a lesson by choosing the most expensive ring she could find!

'Do you see anything you like?' asked the manager. 'We do have more.'

Maggie looked longingly. After all, a ring was just a piece of jewellery. It meant nothing in these circumstances, she supposed. 'They are all lovely,' she said apologetically. She fingered one — a solitaire diamond in an antique setting.

'You like that one, don't you?' said Adam. 'I can tell. Right — we'll have it.'

'Wait a minute!' He rushed her so . . . she just had to put a stop to it. 'Adam dear,' she muttered through her teeth. 'Hadn't you better ask how much it is, first?'

'Certainly not. Nothing but the best for you, darling.' He leaned across the glass counter to whisper playfully to the man there. 'We're not going to tell her the price . . . are we?'

The man beamed. 'No sir. No, Mr Blair, certainly not — if you say so. And may I offer you both my congratulations?'

'You may. And thank you. You can

wrap that up, if you like. I will present it in proper fashion shortly.'

He was enjoying this. Maggie wished she was. She could see that for him it was all a game — even if the purpose behind it was serious — so why not have fun? But it was no fun for her. She had made the fatal mistake of allowing him to get through her defences, and it was hard to know what to do about that now.

A little later she decided that it was best to adopt a flippant attitude to the affair. That was the thing to do — treat the whole thing as a joke, and maybe they would get through it without too much damage, though she doubted it. The damage . . . to her at any rate . . . had already been done.

'Are you going to go down on bended knee, then?' she asked in a mocking tone, as they settled themselves in the small intimate restaurant Adam had chosen for luncheon.

'I very well might,' he replied seriously, handing her the menu. 'Do you want to order?'

She shook her head, and passed it back to him. 'I'll leave it to you.' She was not really hungry, even though she had had precious little to eat during the past two days. So much had been happening. She looked around her at the white clothed tables, each decorated with a tiny bowl of deep blue violas, and was quite content to relax for a while in the comparative peace of the restaurant, and to enjoy the quiet background music.

Adam examined the card. 'I expect Mrs Murphy will do us proud this evening,' he murmured. 'So how about the ham salad?'

Maggie agreed. It would not have mattered to her what the waitress brought them, she hardly noticed what she was eating. Her head was too full of all that had happened. She played with her food, watching Adam tuck into his with great gusto. Trust a man to relish food, no matter what else was happening! Even absorbed as he was, he radiated power and a singleness of purpose that was almost frightening. He was, she knew instinctively, a man with a good appetite for all things . . . food . . . work . . . life . . . love . . .

He looked up. 'You're not slimming are you?' he enquired with such obvious disapproval that it brought a smile to her eyes.

'No. As a matter of fact, this is very nice. It's just that I have rather a lot on my mind.'

He stopped, fork half-way to his mouth. 'Such as . . .?'

She stared at him in amazement. 'Such as!' she exclaimed. 'Such as was it wise to invite us to the house tonight? And how am I going to explain all this to my father, once it's over?'

Adam shrugged, and resumed his meal. 'Is that all? If I hadn't invited you both tonight, it would have looked very strange, don't you think? As for your father, he'll get over it. Broken engagements happen all the time. He won't mind so much when he finds I'm still financing the smallholding.'

Maggie laid down her knife and fork with icy deliberation. She pressed her hands on the starched surface of the tablecloth; it felt stiff and waxy under her fingers. She leaned forward and spoke in a low vehement whisper.

'Foolish my father may be, but I'll tell you this . . . if he knew what was going on he wouldn't accept a penny . . . not a penny . . . '

A smile livened his stern features. 'I can well believe you. But he doesn't know, and you're not going to tell him, are you?' He lifted the bottle of white wine, but Maggie shook her head, so he poured himself another glass, and looked at her over the rim, examining her . . . summing her up. 'I want you to make a good impression tonight. Do you need anything to wear — a dress or something? You can buy whatever you like.'

She felt her temper rising. Who did he think he was, to be so condescending? 'I have my own clothes. You haven't picked me out of the gutter, regardless of what you might think.'

He pushed his plate away and folded his arms, infuriatingly cool. 'I wasn't suggesting I had, Miss Nolan. But, for all that I know, you might have left most of your clothes in London.' His eyes were mocking, daring her to make further protest. 'Mother and Irene like to dress up. I don't wish to make things harder for you.'

She dropped her gaze. What he said was eminently reasonable — he had a habit of putting her in the wrong. 'I see,' she said stiffly. 'I'm sorry. But you needn't worry. I shan't let you down.'

'Did I say I was worrying?'

'You implied it.'

He stretched across the table and took her hand. 'You're wrong there, Maggie. Don't go putting words in my mouth.' That warm look was back in his eyes again, and he began to massage the palm of her hand with the ball of his thumb, sending shivers of pleasure down her spine to her legs which felt as

114

weak as putty. It was so hard . . . so hard to keep up the barriers against him . . . but that was what she had to do. She began to pull away her hand, but he tightened his grip.

'I think this is a suitably romantic place to give you this, don't you?' He brought out the packet she knew contained the ring. Taking it out he slid it onto her finger where it fitted snugly, the diamond winking brightly. 'You do like it, don't you?' His thumb began its caressing again. Maggie bit her lip. Dear Lord — didn't this man realize what he was doing to her?

She swallowed hard. 'It . . . it's beautiful.'

He lifted her hand to his lips. As he lowered his head she found her other hand moving of its own accord towards him. She knew just how the springy thickness of his hair would feel even as she had known how his lips would feel against her hand.

'I think we should get back,' she said faintly. Better go, before she made a complete fool of herself.

Adam looked up quickly. His grip on her fingers increased until it was painful. His eyes darkened. He seemed angry — though she could not imagine why he should be. 'If you wish,' he said curtly.

'I . . . have a lot to do.' The excuse sounded tame, even to her.

He let go of her hand and stood up, pushing his chair back roughly. Then he paid the bill, and they left in silence. All the way back he didn't speak a word. They had nearly reached Ballybrae when they had to slow down for a car coming the other way. Mrs Manson was driving, Adam's mother beside her. Irene pulled up alongside, and wound down her window. Adam did the same.

'You seem to have recovered,' he said.

Irene smiled at him. Her lips made a perfect curve, her teeth showing pearly white between them. She wrinkled her nose playfully. 'Of course. It was only a little travel sickness, darling. You know I hate flying.' Her eyes slid past him to

Maggie. 'You've had a nice morning's shopping?'

The enquiry was perfectly natural, and yet something about it riled Maggie. 'Lovely,' she answered firmly, smiling just as radiantly back at the woman. 'Adam introduced me to this dear little restaurant. I had no idea it had opened.' She snuggled up to him — let him have his money's-worth! 'It was very romantic — wasn't it sweetheart?'

'Hmmm!' His agreement was vehement . . . or was it a cough . . . hard to tell, really? 'Er . . . where are you both going?'

His mother leaned forward to speak past Irene. 'We're going into town to call at house agents.'

'House agents? Whatever for?'

Irene's tongue flicked from between her red lips for a moment, and moistened them. She looked pleased with herself. 'Why to look for a house, Adam dear. After all, I have to live somewhere, and I've taken a liking to it

117

around here. 'Bye darling. 'Bye Miss Nolan. We'll see you tonight, I believe.'

She wound up her window and drove on, smiling. Adam started up the engine, and they continued, still in silence, to Ballybrae. So much for his prediction that Irene Manson would soon get bored and leave. This put quite a different complexion on things. What would he do now? Maggie didn't dare ask him, he was in such a funny mood.

At the cottage Adam unloaded the groceries. The door was not locked — it never was — but there was no sign of her father, though he had banked up the fire. Out telling all his cronies the good news, no doubt! thought Maggie. She got rid of her shawl, and poked the fire back into life.

'If you'd just put that box on the table,' she told him, 'I can sort everything out later.'

'I never realized two people ate so much,' he complained as he kicked the door shut behind him.

'I bet you spend more than this in a

118

single day,' she replied scathingly. 'There's nothing very special here . . . only the bare necessities.' She hesitated, knowing that she did not want him to leave . . . not yet. 'Would you like a coffee before you go?'

'That would be nice. Is there anything I can do?'

She smiled over her shoulder at him. 'I doubt it. But you can make room on the table, if you like. I won't be long.'

When she returned with two earthen mugs of fragrant coffee, she found him in her father's chair, legs stretched out, feet to the fire. Putting the tray in the space he had cleared, she studied him. He had removed his tweed jacket, and even without it his shoulders filled the width of the chair, but he carried no extra weight — there wasn't a hint of surplus fat, only strength in every line of his body, even in the sharp angle of his jaw as he turned his head at her arrival. She felt a throb of familiarity, as if she had been used to seeing him there all her life.

'Let me . . . ' He began to rise.

'No — no. You sit there. Here . . . ' She handed him a mug, and sat opposite him. 'You look tired,' she remarked.

Adam sat for a while, his eyes hooded, thoughtfully sipping his coffee before answering. He gave a faint smile. 'You're a treasure — d'you know that? For one thing, you make damned good coffee. For another, you let a man tell you things in his own good time.'

Remembering how, earlier, she had pushed him for information, she could not agree, but looked at him warily, saying nothing.

'You must be wondering whether Irene means it — about staying in this area.' He leaned forward and gave the fire a poke. 'Heaven knows! But I doubt it. Nothing would induce her to settle so far from the bright lights, and her fashionable friends.'

Maggie still did not reply. She could think of one thing that would keep his ex-wife hanging around! Then Adam seemed to make his mind up about something. He drained his mug, and rose to his feet. 'Get up,' he ordered.

Maggie looked puzzled. He beckoned impatiently. 'Come on.'

Slowly she stood. He held out his hands, and after a moment's hesitation she placed her own in them.

His hazel eyes held hers. He tilted his head back a little, scrutinizing her from under half closed lids. 'Tonight we'll be watched by both mother and Irene. Can you pass the test? Can you convince Irene that she is wasting her time here — that she might as well let me have the shares . . . and go?'

'I . . . I think so.' She saw him frown at her uncertainty. 'Yes I can,' she added defiantly. 'I will.'

He looked sceptical. 'Not the way you've been carrying on.'

'What d'you mean?' Her voice rose indignantly. She thought she'd done rather well, in the car.

He made a sound of disgust. 'You're no actress.'

'I never said I was!'

'Look at you now — edgy as hell — and for what? Just because I'm holding your hands.'

Maggie blushed. 'That's ridiculous . . .' she began.

'You're right — it is.' He drew her even closer. 'We're supposed to be engaged, but you jump away the minute I get near you.'

'I do not!' Her mouth was dry, and her heart had begun to thump an erratic rhythm.

'Don't you?' His eyes gleamed sardonically. He moved his hands to her waist. 'Perhaps we ought to practice. Forget your lost lover for a moment. Let's see what a performance you can give with me.'

A wave of weakness swept over Maggie as he drew her against him. He was asking too much. If she let herself go . . . if she gave in to the demand of the hands that were travelling around her back . . . if she allowed herself to melt as he bent his head to press his lips against her neck . . . she would be lost! She closed her eyes in anguish, hearing his breathing quicken, and arched her neck with a moan as his questing mouth set her senses aflame.

'Maggie . . . ' he muttered thickly. 'Maggie . . . ' Then his lips brushed her cheek, and his mouth claimed hers.

'No . . . no!' She twisted away, unable to endure the sweet cruelty of it any longer.

He gripped her by the shoulders. She was frightened at the anger in his face. 'Damn you, Maggie Nolan — do you have to make it so obvious that you find me repulsive?'

He tried to pull her to him again, but this time, ready for him, she placed her hands against his chest and pushed hard. Taken by surprise he swayed, and the rug skidded out from under his feet. He fell backwards, pulling her with him. Down they went, flat on the floor in front of the fire. She landed on top of him, legs sprawling, her skirt hitched up around her thighs.

The shock took her breath away — but then she raised her head in alarm. He was lying so still. Perhaps she had killed him? But even as the dreadful thought came to her, his broad chest began to heave . . . she was shaken up and down on it. She stared — incredulous. He was laughing! His arms captured her, preventing escape.

'Oh Maggie,' he gasped. 'I didn't mean for you to be that eager!'

A moment of relief, and then she found herself laughing too, her hands clutching the soft white material of his shirt, her face buried in his shoulder. His hand found its way to her head, removing the pins that restrained her hair so that it tumbled around them both, its heavy silkiness curling across his cheek. The movement brought her awareness back to the intimacy of their position, and she tried to shift — but that only made things worse. She found herself looking down into suddenly serious hazel eyes, so close to her own that she could hardly focus on them.

His mouth was only a breath away. Her lips parted, and in a dream she lowered them to his.

It was as she had always known it would be, from the very first time he had touched her. The feel of his mobile mouth under hers made her forget all her good resolutions. What was the use now of worrying about how she would feel once this was over? Over it would be, she knew, and she would have to watch him walk away — thanking her politely, no doubt. But that didn't matter now. Nothing mattered . . .

The kiss went on and on . . . warm . . . sensuous . . . drugging her senses. His mouth was gently insistent, claiming hers, demanding more and more response, until she could have died with the ecstasy of it. Then he rolled her to one side, his arm cradling her head, their bodies still welded together, the fire warm against her back. He began exploring her face with soft teasing kisses . . . her eyes . . . the corners of her mouth. She could not bear it for a moment longer, and with a moan blindly groped to bring that teasing mouth back to her own. The tip of his tongue gently slid along her lips, and something exploded inside. With a gasp her lips parted to grant him entry.

And then his hands took over. They slid beneath her sweater, and she felt his touch on the bare skin of her back, and pressed against him — instinctively wanting that touch on the whole of her body. Never had she felt like this. She was swept away with an aching desire to be at one with him, her nipples hardened with anticipation . . .

Crash! A car door slammed. Singing . . . the sound of feet. Then . . .

'Oh, there you are . . . hic. Thass nice! Havin' a nice cuddle in front of the fire. Oh yesh . . . thass ver' ver' nice, that is!'

'Da!'

Somehow Adam found his way to his

feet, shielding Maggie as she frantically straightened her clothing. Bonnie Nolan stood in the doorway grinning foolishly, waving a whiskey flask in his hand. He looked on owlishly as Adam grabbed his jacket from the chair.

'I approve,' he told them solemnly. 'Glad to see you two . . . hic . . . love-birds. I've been . . . celebrating.'

'Er . . . Hmmm!' Adam cleared his throat. Maggie felt hysterical laughter bubbling. She couldn't bring herself to look at him. She buried her head in her arms.

'I . . . er . . . I'd better be going now,' he said stiffly. 'I'll see you later Mr Nolan. Maggie . . . er . . . there'll be no need to practice, in future.'

He dashed out. Maggie still sat on the floor, her arms around her knees, her head down. She didn't know what she felt. She didn't know whether to laugh or cry. Her father wobbled forward and flopped into the chair Adam had so recently vacated. She peered at him shyly from beneath the black curls that hung down over her forehead.

'I'm happy for you, Maggie,' he uttered solemnly. 'He's a fine man. 'Deed he is. Didn't like him at first, you know.' He took another swig at the flask. 'Main thing ish . . . is . . . you love him. Don' need to ask that, do I . . . or you wouldn't both be rollin' round on my hearth-rug, eh?'

Maggie raised her head to look at her father as he beamed drunkenly at her. Then she ran her hands through her dishevelled hair, and dropped her head back, showing the long line of her throat. Her very skin felt vibrant, alive. Her mouth was soft and swollen from Adam's kisses. She felt foolish . . . languorous . . . wonderful . . . frightened . . . and utterly miserable, all at the same time. Adam had shown exactly how he felt — embarrassed by the whole episode. His parting words had shown quite clearly that he intended there should be no repeat. Oh, he had been carried away by the moment — no doubt about that, but it would never happen again. It had meant nothing to him.

'Oh yes, Da,' she said softly. 'I love him all right.' So help me, she thought, I do. And what am I going to do about it?

5

It was a mistake to be going there at all, Maggie thought that evening, as they drove to the Big House. She had spent the remainder of the afternoon making the both of them presentable. She had poured numerous black coffees for Bonnie while she sponged and pressed his suit; it was dark grey, and though shiny at the knees and elbows, it was the best he had. He should by rights be wearing a dinner jacket — but that was out of the question, and she had to do the best she could with a clean white shirt and black tie. She didn't have the heart to take him to task for coming home the worse for drink. If the truth be known she felt too awkward to bring the matter up, considering the compromising position in which he had found his only daughter. She was only thankful he had not come home a few minutes later, or it might have been very much worse.

She grew uncomfortably warm at the thought of it. How could she look Adam Blair in the face when they met again? It was not that she was ashamed. She had fallen in love, and she was not afraid to let her body follow where her heart had already gone . . . if he had but loved her too. But he didn't. He had only been using her, forcing a reaction from her to suit his own purposes. She bit her lip. Well — he was probably very pleased with her response, then.

'Here we are,' said Maggie at last. 'Da, are you all right now?'

'Maggie . . . will you not keep on at me, there's a good girl. I'm perfectly sober.'

In the light that shone from the lamp outside the front door she looked at him affectionately, and brushed a strand of cotton from his lapel. 'You look very smart.'

'You look a treat yourself,' he answered.

Maggie certainly hoped so. She had, after much deliberation, piled her hair into a froth of curls on top of her head. It looked sophisticated, she thought, going well with her freshly laundered high-necked white office blouse, and her long black skirt nipped in at her slender waist by a red belt. The hair style accentuated her high cheekbones and wide-spaced eyes. She felt quite pleased with the effect. Good enough even for Mr Adam Blair — which was just as well, for in spite of her haughty words, these were the only clothes she owned that were suitable for evening wear. Malcolm had not been a great one for taking her out — he had told her he resented any minutes not spent alone with her — and she had believed him, more fool her, though she now realized he had merely been avoiding discovery.

However, when they were ushered into the sitting room, and Maggie saw

Irene Manson perched on the arm of Adam's chair, her satisfaction with her own appearance was short-lived. Irene was wearing a short red chiffon dress — a wispy creation of flame that revealed an elegant length of nyloned legs which ended in incredibly high-heeled strapped sandals. Well — Adam had warned her. She should have taken him up on his offer, and bought something new.

He looked undeniably handsome, and in some indefinable way different, dressed as he was in a dinner jacket that fitted his muscular frame like a glove. Maggie's throat was dry with nerves, but she held out her hands, presenting her mouth for a kiss; she was not going to give him reason for accusing her of holding back. But, strangely, it was Adam whose lips felt reluctant. His hands clasped hers, but he made no attempt to draw her closer.

'Darling, come in,' he said smoothly. 'Mr Nolan, let me introduce you to everyone.'

Her father disposed of, Adam drew her to one side. 'I owe you an apology,' he said tersely. His gaze was focussed somewhere over her left shoulder. He cleared his throat. 'For this afternoon.' His voice was so low, that only she could hear. 'I never intended . . . I didn't mean . . . anyway, I apologize. It won't happen again.'

For the benefit of those watching, Maggie gave him a loving smile. 'That's quite all right,' she muttered coldly. 'It didn't mean a thing.' What had she been expecting anyway . . . that he would rush to her, and want to start where he had left off?

'Your father . . . did he say anything?'

Maggie stared at him. He really was extremely embarrassed. The great Adam Blair, so sure of himself, and here he was acting like a Lord of the Manor caught with the kitchen maid.

'You needn't worry,' she answered dryly. 'He hasn't come armed with a shotgun. As a matter of fact, he thought it very romantic.'

'Oh,' said Adam. 'That's a relief.' He smiled for the first time, but she turned away, hurt by his desire to wipe out what had happened. She knew it meant nothing to him — but did he have to make that quite so obvious? In the general welter of conversation someone offered her a dry sherry, and she clutched the glass thankfully. In comparison with Irene she felt gauche and over-dressed, and the exchange with Adam had not exactly helped her self-esteem.

Adam drew her to one side. 'Relax, Maggie — you look lovely.'

She was not mollified. She supposed she should be grateful for his vote of confidence, but she had seen the way Irene's arm had been resting along the back of his chair, touching those broad shoulders — how his face had been turned to hers. Perhaps he was already regretting embarking on this stupid deception.

'Thank you,' she said shortly. 'But I know I can't compete with present company.' Not even with his mother, she thought, watching Mrs Blair in her stylish black, relieved only by the expensive jewellery she always wore. Her Da did not seem overawed, though. He was entertaining the lady with anecdotes that seemed to amuse . . . even Irene was listening. Bonnie could charm the birds off the trees when he felt like it — and if he was sober!

'Maggie . . . ' Adam claimed her attention again. He gently touched her upswept hair. 'You can hold your own, don't you know that?'

Even with Irene? she longed to ask, but was wise enough to hold her tongue. She knew the answer to that one, 'Let's be honest,' she said impatiently, 'if you *had* bought my outfit, what would you have chosen? Something slinky and revealing, I suppose!'

He laughed. 'On the contrary,' he said steadily, his eyes holding hers, 'I think it best to cover you up as much as possible.'

He made her sound as exciting as a brown paper parcel. Not that she'd have wanted to wear a sexy dress — but perversely she would have liked him to want her to.

Irene heard Adam's laugh, as if she was tuned in to him, aware of his every movement, every tone of his voice. She glided across and linked her arm through his. 'I can't let you be monopolized,' she purred. 'You don't mind do you, Miss Nolan . . . or may I call you Maggie? Such a lovely name, so . . . rustic!' Her eyes were cold. Maggie was beginning to revise her opinion of Adam's ex-wife.

At that moment Mrs Murphy announced that dinner was served and Bonnie Nolan offered his arm to Mrs Blair with a courtly gesture. Irene was still holding on to Adam, and showed every intention of continuing to do so, leaving Maggie standing alone — but Adam was quick to rectify the situation, and, offering his other arm to Maggie, they moved together to the dining room.

The meal was delicious. Mrs Murphy had, as Adam had predicted, done them proud, with mouth-watering tender lamb, and fresh vegetables new-picked from the estate. The roast potatoes were crisp and golden, the gravy beyond praise, and the wine that Adam poured was mellow and relaxing. Under its influence even Mrs Blair was being affable. Adam was attentive, as befitted a man engaged to be married. He was playing his part well, thought Maggie wryly, even if he *was* feeling sorry he had ever started this, But he was equally attentive to Irene. Not that she was jealous . . . after all, if it hadn't been for his ex-wife, she would not be there at all.

'You didn't really come over here just to settle down?' Adam was asking Irene. 'So come along — what was your real reason?' He was smiling, teasing even. Maggie could feel her own face growing stiff with the polite smile she had pasted there.

'Darling,' purred Irene. 'do you need to ask that? I discovered who was buying up Charles's shares . . . and why.' There was triumph in those green eyes. She tore a piece off her bread roll, and gave Adam a sly sideways look. 'You really need Charles's firm, don't you?'

'In the event of a takeover your shares would double in value. You'd stand to make a packet,' Adam pointed out calmly.

'Well . . . ' she gave a calculating smile. 'We'll just have to see.'

'How long do you intend staying over here?' asked Maggie.

There was a hush — one of those silences that occur at dinner parties. It had been quite an innocent remark, and yet it came out sounding ungracious. Maggie brazened it out, looking down as she cut her meat, and then glancing back at Irene with a polite look of interest. 'I don't somehow imagine our rural surroundings to be quite your cup of tea.'

For a second Irene's mask of perfection seemed to slip. An expression of fury crossed her face, but she soon had it under control. 'On the contrary!' Her laughter tinkled out. 'After the hectic life I've led for the past few years I welcome peace and quiet.' She turned her great eyes on Adam. 'When Charles died I found he had made many rash investments. I need help and advice, if I'm to survive at all.'

'Are you really thinking about buying a house here?' Maggie persisted.

Irene looked at her with ill-disguised dislike. 'Yes,' she said acidly. 'Why not? I must live somewhere.'

She meant it, Maggie had no doubt of that. She looked at Adam, but he did not react. Perhaps he didn't care any more. Perhaps, now that the initial shock of his ex-wife's arrival had worn off, he didn't find her presence so disturbing? The idea was depressing.

These thoughts were interrupted by Mrs Murphy's arrival with a meringue dessert that was a masterpiece of engineering, and the conversation returned to more general matters.

'I didn't realize you were seeing over this house for the first time, when we arrived,' said Adam's mother, as they were drinking their coffee. 'Somehow I imagined that you and Adam met here.'

'No, we met in London,' he cut in. 'In fact, Maggie only arrived back here yesterday.'

'Well then,' said Mrs Blair graciously, 'I'll show you around, while the men can smoke if they wish and talk business.'

Maggie joined her with some misgivings, wondering if this was a ploy, to get her alone in order to ask questions she could not answer. But Adam's mother seemed to be making a genuine effort to be nice, and so the least she could do was to respond. At least Irene had not offered to accompany them, disappearing on some business of her own.

Maggie had never before penetrated further than the hallway of the Big House, and even that was greatly changed. As Mrs Blair led her from room to room Maggie could see Adam's influence in the feeling of spaciousness and light, brought about by the harmonious blending of pastel colours. She liked the generously proportioned rooms with their high ceilings, and the choice of contrasting fabrics. It was an uncluttered house, light and peaceful, the plain walls relieved by colourful paintings — many of them originals.

Mrs Blair opened a bedroom door. 'Of course, this is Adam's.'

Maggie nodded. There could be no mistaking the identity of the owner. It was such a masculine room, that she would have known it was his, even if his jacket had not been slung over a chair back. There was a double bed. She wondered if he had ever shared it with Irene, and then realized that she had been gone long before he acquired this house. She mentally kicked herself for even thinking such a thing.

'It's a lovely house,' she said truthfully.

Adam's mother led the way back down the wide staircase. 'Yes, it is. Of course, Seamus didn't take much interest in it. Adam has worked very hard.' She added confidentially, 'I always thought he was preparing the house in the hope that he and Irene . . .'

She stopped at the foot of the stairs and turned, gripping Maggie's arm with her bejewelled hand. Her eyes were sharp and bright, but not unkind. 'Perhaps I shouldn't have said that.'

What was she to say? When she answered her own voice sounded too bright and brittle to her ears. 'It's quite all right. I can understand how you hoped . . .' her words tailed away.

'I'm so glad.' His mother smiled. 'I would hate to hurt you, my dear. I must admit that perhaps I was a little abrupt yesterday. It was such a surprise, you see, and . . . well . . .'

'I didn't make a very good impression,' said Maggie ruefully.

Mrs Blair laughed. 'At least you made a very muddy one.' She indicated a door at the back of the hallway. 'Have you seen Adam's new conference extension? He designed it for his business. If you are to be working with him no doubt you'll see it in use soon.'

The room they entered was long and wide and ran the whole length of the back of the house. It was empty, apart from a large conference table at one end. The floor was highly polished, and the lofty ceiling raftered. The far wall consisted entirely of curtained windows. Mrs Blair crossed the room and pulled a cord. The curtains drew back silently, and one section of the glass panels slid aside.

'Swimming pool and sauna,' she said almost disapprovingly. 'I suppose it's to relax Adam's flagging executives, though of course swimming has always been Adam's sport, and he uses it every morning.'

Another touch of Adam's single-minded genius! A charming indoor patio area was screened by plants and contained comfortable loungers, and the pool's water lapped blue against the ceramic tiles of the surround. She could imagine him swimming. That would account for his muscular shoulders. He would look good in swimming trunks . . .

'He should certainly be able to clinch business deals here,' she exclaimed, to divert her thoughts from the highly erotic line they were taking. 'I suppose he intends this house as a centre for business contacts?'

'Hasn't he discussed it with you, then?'

Mrs Blair's voice was sharply inquisitive. Just the kind of trap Maggie had been expecting, and even so she'd fallen for it.

'Oh yes,' she retaliated calmly. 'He told me. But it's quite different when you see the real thing.'

'Yes . . . ' Adam's mother turned to

leave. 'I expect you found Irene different from what you expected too.' She shut the glass panel behind them, and drew the curtain. 'He adored her, you know.'

'I guessed as much.' Maggie ran her tongue across lips suddenly dry.

'Oh yes, he worshipped her. He never told me what happened, but from things Irene let slip, he treated her very badly. Nevertheless, I thought he still . . . but there, obviously, my dear, I was wrong.'

His mother had done just what she intended, Maggie thought bleakly. Under that friendly facade had been the determination to point out exactly where they all stood. If this had been a real engagement the seeds of doubt would have been well and truly sown. Well, she's wasting her time, she thought with grim humour. Adam was paying for a fiancée, and that was what he was going to get — until he himself released her from the bargain. And that might be sooner than she had imagined. It couldn't be too soon for her! Fate, she reflected, had played her a mean hand. Adam needed her, but only to act a part. But why? Was he really only interested in Irene's casting vote — or was he, as his mother had hinted, deep down still in love with his ex-wife?

Irene was waiting for them in the sitting room, engulfed in an armchair, her blonde head in sharp contrast to the dark leather, her slender legs crossed elegantly. She smiled as they entered, and a significant glance passed between her and Adam's mother.

'What . . . the men not here yet?'

'No,' she drawled. 'You know what Adam is like, nothing gets in the way of business. Never mind. It gives me time to have a little chat with Maggie.'

'Yes. In that case I will leave you both for a while, I have a few things to do. I won't be long.'

Mrs Blair retreated. Irene extended a hand and offered a silver cigarette case. 'D'you smoke?'

Maggie shook her head. She sat in the chair facing Irene.

'No . . . somehow I didn't think you would.' Irene extracted a cigarette, slim fingers picking it out, lighting it. She leaned back her head, breathing out the smoke. Her eyes narrowed. 'It won't work, you know.'

Maggie raised her eyebrows. She was not going to be drawn. 'What won't?' she asked innocently. Was she mistaken, or was there a flush of temper on those perfect features? But Irene smiled. She had little teeth. Small and perfect. And no doubt sharp, like a cat's.

'This silly business with you and Adam.'

'Silly?' Maggie allowed herself to look mildly surprised. 'I'm sorry, but I don't consider being engaged to be married silly.'

Irene sprang to her feet, the red chiffon flaring. She paced angrily about the room. 'You know very well what I mean. Adam hasn't taken me in for a moment. The whole thing is preposterous. He doesn't love you. How could he . . . it's impossible!'

'Oh?' Maggie's voice remained steady, in contrast to the other's agitated tones. 'How d'you make that out?'

Irene looked at her scornfully. 'Just look at you,' she sneered. 'Sitting there so prim and proper. Adam is a real man . . . virile . . . passionate. He needs a woman who can love him back . . . '

'He didn't complain this afternoon.'

She never knew what made her say it, but it had the desired effect. Irene stood with her mouth open, the tirade stopped mid-stream.

'You mean . . . ?'

'Yes,' said Maggie. 'I do. Not that it's any of your business.' May God forgive me for the lie, she thought. But then, it might not have been a lie, if Da had not come home so soon.

'I don't believe you!' Irene stood over Maggie. Small though she was, she exuded menace, and Maggie felt her scalp prickle.

'I don't really care whether you do, or not,' she retorted, 'You were married to Adam once, and you left him. What he does now is not your concern.'

'No! He loves me. He'll always love me. And I want him back.' Irene spat out the words.

'What a pity you ever left him, then,' retorted Maggie. She swung on her heel to leave the room, but Irene caught hold of her.

'And do you know why I went? Did Adam ever tell you?'

Maggie hesitated.

'Ah yes. You didn't know, did you?' Irene's beautiful face was ugly to see, contorted with malicious triumph. 'He didn't tell you I couldn't give him the child he wanted. Because of an operation, you see. *That* was why I left with Charles. Adam needed his freedom — and I had to have someone. Charles was good to me.'

Tears welled up in those big green eyes. 'Deep down nothing has changed,' she whispered. 'Adam is a very attractive man. There have been many women in his life . . . but he belongs to me. I was wrong to leave . . . but now I can put that right. I know he still wants me. Can you marry him, knowing that?'

The walls seemed to be closing in. *This has nothing to do with me*, something inside Maggie cried. But that was not so. It had everything to do with her. If it was true, then once more she was standing between a man and the wife who loved him. Heaven help her — she didn't want any more on her conscience . . . but she had made a bargain . . . given her promise.

'I'm sorry,' she cried desperately, 'but what happened between you and Adam was a long time ago.'

Irene's face resumed its expression of malice. 'Don't say I didn't warn you,' she hissed. 'I have the one thing Adam needs — Charles's shares. Without my vote his takeover will fail.' She laughed, a cruel brittle laugh. 'Adam will do anything for Blairs of Devon. You'll learn.'

To Maggie's profound relief the confrontation was ended by the return of the menfolk. 'I'm sorry we've been so long. Bonnie and I were deep in plans for the future of the smallholding.' Adam held out his arms. 'Did you miss me?' More play acting, but his eyes were searching, making Maggie wonder if he knew the sort of things Irene had been saying. He closed his arms about her protectively.

'It seemed like an eternity,' she admitted, and she meant it. But she looked over Adam's shoulder and saw the hatred in Irene's eyes. Irene *did* believe her . . . but it would not stop her for one moment, of that Maggie was sure. Irene wanted Adam, and would not rest until he was hers once more.

6

'Good morning. Ready for work then?' Mrs Murphy took Maggie's coat, and hung it in the cloakroom. 'Mr Blair isn't in the office yet, but he said for you to go along in.'

'Good — thank you.'

Surely nobody had ever started work in stranger circumstances. Maggie smoothed her dark hair, neatly arranged in a knot at her neck. 'That was a lovely meal you cooked for us last night.'

'Did you think so?' Mrs Murphy beamed. 'And Bonnie — did he enjoy himself too?'

Maggie's lips twisted in a wry smile. 'Oh yes, he had a wonderful time.' Indeed, her father had. Only that morning at breakfast he had told her so, though it was a wonder he remembered, the amount of drink he'd put away. Still, he'd done her proud — and she was pleased one of them had enjoyed the evening.

'I'm glad of that.' The housekeeper's eyes focussed on Maggie's ring. 'Can I see? Oh, it's a beauty sure enough. I'm happy for you Maggie, and I know your mother would be if she was here, God rest her.'

Maggie escaped into the office as quickly as she could, closed the door behind her, and leaned against it with a sigh of relief. All night long she had lain sleepless, reliving the events of the previous day. Oh Adam — if he only knew the havoc he had wreaked, just when she had thought she was getting her life together. They had become torture to her, those melting looks that meant nothing, his touch that had the power to turn her bones to water. All very well for him, she thought bitterly. He could blow hot and cold whenever it suited him. He could set her senses alight, and then apologize . . . apologize for what she thought they had both found special. That was the most hurtful thing of all. However — in here Adam would simply be her employer. No need for either of them to pretend. In this office he would certainly expect a different value for money . . . the money Da owed him . . . so she had better become familiar with everything before he arrived. She smoothed her brown linen skirt. It toned well with her plain cream wool jumper. Make a good impression on your first day in a new job the Commercial College had insisted. She doubted if they'd ever come across a situation like this.

There was nothing to personalize the room at all. Maggie made a mental note to bring in some flowers to brighten the place up, and a mirror . . . a girl certainly needed a mirror. She sat down at the desk that was to be hers and switched on the typewriter; it buzzed and shot back to the margin in readiness. So far so good. She plugged in the word processor, approving of its clear green display that was easy on the eyes, and checked the audio machine.

There was nothing else she could do until Adam put in an appearance. Perhaps he was still having breakfast. She imagined the cosy scene of Adam and Irene eating toast together, and shied uncomfortably from the idea. Restlessly she wandered to the window. Outside there was a wide stone patio with steps leading down to a sweeping lawn. How she would have enjoyed working here, close to him, if things had been different. Strange to think that she had, by a quirk of fate, landed this job. She wondered with a smile of amusement what Malcolm would say if he knew.

The door opened and Adam pushed his way through, his arms full of document files. His face was thunderous. He dumped them on her desk, and moved away to the grey metal filing cabinet for more. Maggie returned to her typist's chair and waited quietly, her hands in her lap.

'Good morning, Mr Blair,' she said, determined that he should have no cause to accuse her of taking advantage of an intimacy that only existed for the purpose of deceiving others.

''Morning,' he said abruptly. He dropped two more files and two audio tapes onto her desk. 'There's enough dictation to keep you going for a while. Just work your way through these. If you have any problems, let me know.'

He turned away and sat at his desk, picking up the post that lay there. He began slitting open envelopes with a paper knife . . . looking as though he'd as soon slit her throat. Now what had she done? He had seemed perfectly happy last night when she'd left. If anyone was irritable it should be herself, after the night she'd spent tortured by memories of their love-making beside the fire. She had fully intended keeping their relationship professional — a straightforward working partnership and no more — but now that he was making it so brutally clear he desired the same she felt perversely disappointed. With a sigh she slipped one of the tapes into the audio machine, and plugged in her ear phones. Adam's voice came over clearly. 'Take a letter to the local authority . . .'

He was engrossed in reading his mail. He was not dressed for the part; his old brown corduroys and Aran sweater had seen better days . . . but they suited him. They emphasized his rugged looks, hinting at the power of the body they concealed — a power she knew only too well. Although he appeared to be relaxed, the set of his body betrayed an air of tension. The morning sunshine fell sideways across him, highlighting the craggy lines of his profile. His mouth was shut like a clamp, and she had already come to know that as a sign of displeasure. His forehead was creased in a frown — though why he should be feeling bad-tempered she could not imagine . . . perhaps he was always like this at work. If so, all the better. An ill-tempered boss she could cope with. He looked incredibly tough, but she could be tough too. He'd find that out.

She turned back to her work, and soon her fingers were flying over the keys, and she became so absorbed that she did not look up until he interrupted her with a loud cough.

He glowered at her. 'Must you make such a din?'

Her grey eyes widened. 'If you want me to type with no sound at all I suggest you'd better move me into another room.'

'Hmmm.' He looked her over, and she was glad she had chosen her clothes carefully ... though if his expression was anything to go by she might as well have turned up in jeans with her hair dyed purple.

'Is that all?' she asked quietly.

'No!' He swivelled his chair to face her. His mouth was pulled down at the corners, his eyes brooding. 'What were you smiling about when I came in?' he asked abruptly.

Maggie stared — it had come to something when she had to account for her every thought. 'When you came in? Oh . . . I was thinking of Malcolm,' she began truthfully. 'If you want to know . . .'

'I don't,' he interrupted. He rose from his seat in a sudden forceful movement, as if he could no longer bear to remain still. 'Your love life is no concern of mine.'

She had been about to explain about her previous firm. Perhaps he even knew Malcolm . . . but his curt remark hurt.

'I'm glad to hear that, Mr Blair,' she said icily, and picked up her earphones again.

'I'm going down to Ballybrae,' he said brusquely before she could start typing. 'I've got to send the men down with the tractor for your father. I may as well go now. I can't concentrate here.'

She was stung by his reminder of her indebtedness to him. Had he really meant to rub in the fact that she was there out of his charity, and had to dance to whatever tune he chose to play?

'Are you always like this in the mornings?' she asked with her usual forthrightness. 'Or is it me? Have I done something wrong?'

His hand was already on the door handle, but he looked back at her with eyes that were an icy gleam under their heavy lids. 'Oh no,' he grated. 'I just love discovering at breakfast that you've broadcast the details of our lovemaking to all and sundry.'

'I've what!' The picture of Adam and Irene sharing a breakfast table returned in all its vivid intimacy.

'D'you deny that you told my ex-wife what happened yesterday afternoon — embroidering it considerably, by all accounts?' His mouth twisted sardonically. 'Perhaps it gives you a kick.'

She jumped to her feet. 'I did nothing of the kind,' she flared. 'How dare you suggest such a thing.'

'But you admit you told her we made love?'

161

'Well . . . yes,' she stammered, her cheeks scarlet. 'But that was all I said. And there was a good reason.'

He folded his arms, with a contemptuous sneer. 'I can't wait!'

Her temper exploded. She stalked up to him and wagged an angry finger under his nose. 'I was doing what you were paying me for Mr High and Mighty Blair. I was protecting you. She guessed our engagement was a sham . . . what did you want me to do, agree with her? She said it must be, because . . . because . . . ' Her voice faltered away.

'Go on.'

Maggie gulped, then, hands on hips, blurted out defiantly. 'She said you couldn't want me because I wasn't sexy enough.'

His expression didn't change, except that if anything a darker look of anger came into his face, hardening the thrust of his jaw.

'And you felt you must prove otherwise?'

162

Maggie looked away, her anger spent. 'It seemed the only thing to do at the time,' she answered in a small voice.

'Hmmm.' That was his only comment. Then he turned to go, but she couldn't leave it like that. There was something she had to know, and she could think of no diplomatic way to put it.

'Is it true Irene can't have a child, because of an operation?'

He swung around to face her, eyes wide, the pupils dark. For a moment she was afraid that he was about to unleash the full force of his fury against her, but he visibly fought down his anger.

'Yes.' He gave a short harsh laugh. 'Quite a night for mutual confidences, it seems — though I'm surprised she told you that.'

So it was true. Perhaps the rest of the things Irene had said were equally true . . . that deep down he loved her . . . that he wanted her still. Maggie's shoulders drooped and she turned to her desk.

'Thank you. I won't keep you any longer, Mr Blair.'

Two strides and he was at her side, gripping her arms so tightly that it hurt. 'Stop calling me that,' he rasped. 'It sounds ridiculous. Are you deliberately trying to annoy me?'

She strained away from him. 'But I thought here . . . in the office I'm only your secretary.'

'You are my fiancée.' He emphasized each word deliberately. 'Here or anywhere else. That was the agreement. You wear my ring. Do I make myself clear?'

'Perfectly!' Defiant though she was, Maggie's mouth trembled, and his dark gaze fixed on the full ripeness of her lips.

'Then prove it . . . '

'You haven't bought me completely,' she gasped, but her words were cut short as his mouth plundered hers. She pushed against him, but his kiss demanded compliance, and she felt a swirling dizziness as her own lips weakly parted. This was no gentle teasing kiss. This was the harsh demand of a man who was claiming his own; her senses recognized the validity of that claim. Of their own volition her arms reached up to wind around his neck, and he pulled her even closer.

Her blood was on fire. His fingers caressed the nape of her neck, sending shivers of delight down her spine, and she pressed against him in an abandonment of delight, her breathing quickening in rhythm with his, lost in a timeless ecstasy, conscious only of the feel of him, the taste and touch and warmth of him. What is happening to me? she thought desperately, knowing she had never before wanted a man as she wanted Adam. Her previous experience with Malcolm counted for nothing, swept away as though it had never been, bringing her to this moment new and vulnerable, thirsty for the experience as the land thirsted for the summer rain.

She was unprepared and shocked when he thrust her away from him. For a moment he stood staring at her, unsmiling, and she stared back, her eyes huge in a face grown pale, her lips still parted, her breasts heaving as she drew in a shuddering breath. Then he slammed out of the room without giving her so much as a backward glance.

Dumbly she felt behind her for her chair, and collapsed into it. Her fingers crept up to touch her lips, still bruised and throbbing from the pressure of his mouth, and her eyes filled with tears. What was he trying to prove? she thought angrily. That she was completely in his power? That much was evident, he didn't need to punish her for it. Or was it pent-up frustration caused by having Irene under the same roof?

'I'm damned if he'll use me as a substitute!' She picked up her headphones once more, and began to type with vicious speed. 'That's the last time he'll treat me like that!' But she knew that if he took her in his arms again she would respond in just the same way. She could not help herself. It was no use. There was no way she could go through with this now, and she would tell him so when he returned. There must be some other way to pay back Da's debt.

She got through the morning by working with fanatical concentration, giving herself no opportunity to think of anything else. At one o'clock Mrs Murphy came in to say that Adam was out, but that she was expected to join the family for lunch. The thought of another meal time with Mrs Blair and Irene filled her with dismay, and she pleaded that she was far too busy. Mrs Murphy took pity on her, and fetched a tray loaded with cold chicken, Russian salad, brown rolls, and the remains of the previous night's meringue. Maggie pulled her chair over to the window and sat looking out, while she ate. Now that she had decided on her course of action, she felt calmer, though she was not looking forward to telling Adam that she was backing out of their agreement.

She did not see Adam again until that afternoon, when he strode back into the office bringing with him the fresh coldness of the open air, and the scent of the outdoors. He was still looking angry, but in a different kind of way — more irritated than anything.

'Where the hell's Bonnie?' he demanded.

She stopped typing. 'Da? I don't know. He was supposed to be at home, he was looking forward to seeing the new tractor.'

Adam raked an impatient hand through his hair. 'That's what I thought, but there's been no sign of him. Never mind — it doesn't really matter. I've left a couple of men there to carry on with things. Just as well he's out of the way, really.' He flung himself into his big swivel chair, and looked at her enquiringly. 'How have you got on?

Managed all right?'

So he was going to pretend nothing had happened . . . or perhaps it meant so little to him that it had already slipped his mind. 'I've finished all you left me,' she said stiffly, placing a wire basket of letters in front of him. 'These are ready for you to sign, and copies of the draft memoranda you wanted are on your desk.'

He began signing the letters, writing his name with a bold flourish. At first he read each one through carefully, but then he began to speed up. 'Good,' he said when he had finished. 'In fact . . . very good. You're going to be a great help to me, Maggie.'

At first his approval warmed her, and his smile weakened her resolve — but she fought off the feeling. 'No, Adam!'

He laid down his pen, and the familiar shuttered look closed his expression. 'And what do you mean by that?'

She clenched her fists into tight balls in her lap, and swallowed nervously, looking away from him. 'I mean I'm sorry, but I can't go through with this. I'll find some other way. I'll get work in Duncow, or even travel to Cork . . . and I'll let you have every penny of my wages. I'm . . . I'm sorry.'

He bent his head, and carried on signing the remaining letters. When he had finished he returned the basket to her desk. 'You can post those on your way home. I'll let you off early — you'll want time to make yourself beautiful for the party.'

'Party?' said Maggie blankly — hadn't he been listening to a word she said?

'Our engagement party, darling. The one your father kindly arranged. I'll pick you up at about eight-thirty.'

Her deep breath failed to quell the nervous fluttering in her stomach. 'You don't understand, Adam. There'll be no party. It's over, our little pretence. I'm pulling out.'

A smile played around his mouth. 'It's you who doesn't understand,

Maggie,' he said silkily. 'If you break our bargain, then the agreement is over, and I demand payment in full . . . now.'

She caught her breath. 'You wouldn't,' she breathed. But she knew he would. She could read it in every line of his face, in his eyes as hard as cold steel. He was ruthless — that's why he was so successful . . . wasn't business a jungle where the prize went to the strongest? And that's what he was — a ruthless, predatory beast. If she thwarted him he would wreak his vengeance on Da.

'Why?' she cried in anguish. 'What good is it doing? I'm sure Irene knows the truth. What pleasure are you getting out of this?'

'That,' he said calmly, 'is my business. Now — which is it to be, Maggie? Is your father to have his new tractor, and the help of my men and all he needs for next year's sowing . . . or do I tell my solicitors to call in the debt? It's up to you.'

She sat in silence, hatred blazing in

her eyes. He smiled and walking across to her, patted her on the shoulder. 'That's a good girl, but you'd better look a little more loving tonight. And don't forget to post those letters.'

He sauntered out of the room with that long lazy gait of his, and left her glaring after him. She sat like that for a long time, until she suddenly whirled around and banged her clenched fists on the desk. Damn him, damn him, damn him! Her father had been right after all — she was caught in a trap, and the worst thing was that it did nothing to lessen the way she felt about him.

'Did I hear Adam leaving?'

Only Irene could drawl in such a way that the most innocent remark sounded insulting.

'What do you want?' Maggie asked bluntly, turning to face the intruder.

Irene raised her eyebrows, and sauntered across the room in a haze of heavy perfume. 'My dear, I was curious. I just had to see where Adam's business went on . . . and how you fitted in.'

'Well, now you've seen,' said Maggie. 'Now, if you don't mind, I don't want to seem inhospitable, but I have work to do.'

Irene gave a faint mocking smile, and perched on the broad window ledge, swinging one dainty foot. She tilted her blonde head. 'Poor Maggie. You know, Adam isn't being fair, involving you in his silly games. Oh . . . you needn't think I don't know what's going on. It was a shock to him when I turned up out of the blue, and he needed time to recover. You were just a smoke screen, to pretend he didn't need me.'

She was right . . . spot on, in fact. Oh, she was no fool! 'Do you really think,' said Maggie calmly, 'that I would become engaged to a man I didn't love? Why should I do such a thing?'

Irene hesitated. 'I don't know . . . yet,' she murmured. Then, just as Maggie was feeling hopeful that she had saved the day, she continued, 'But I'm working on it. Unless . . . ' Her eyes narrowed. 'Unless you are in love with

Adam.' She gave a harsh laugh that grated on Maggie's nerves. 'That would be a joke, wouldn't it? Poor Maggie! Never mind, it will soon be over — and just as well. It wouldn't do, you must realize that. You're just not in Adam's class. In any case, he's getting used to having me around again. We are reaching an . . . understanding.'

She rose to her feet and swayed her way out. 'I just thought you ought to know,' she purred. ' 'Bye for now.'

'Cat!' said Maggie vehemently to the closed door. After a while she folded the letters, slipped them into their envelopes, and sealed and stamped them. There was nothing else she could do . . . and at least she would have the satisfaction of doing her job properly. Then, gathering them up, she left and drove back to Ballybrae, slipping the post into the pillar box at the end of the lane.

'Da! Where on earth have you been?'

Maggie felt she had every right to be

annoyed. Since returning from the Big House she had, in a flurry of mind-numbing activity, cleaned and polished the whole cottage, prepared a good nourishing stew, taken a bath and washed her hair, and then — still in her dressing gown — eaten her meal on her own, growing all the time more worried as to where here father could be. And now he walked in, when it was almost time for Adam to collect her, flushed and excited, and as bouncy as a rubber ball.

'Have you seen the new tractor, eh Maggie? Isn't she a beauty? I can't wait to get my hands on her . . . have you seen the keys?'

Maggie pointed to the sideboard. 'They're there, but you needn't think you're going out on it now. Da . . . you were supposed to be here when it arrived this morning. Where were you?' She looked critically at his flushed cheeks. 'You've been drinking.'

Bonnie Nolan looked guilty. 'Ah now, Maggie — you sound worse than a wife. Sure, and I only had a little one with Mickey.'

'Mickey from the racetrack?' Her insides lurched. 'Da . . . you haven't been to the races again?'

He grew truculent. 'And why not? They didn't need me here at all, and Mickey knew of a dead cert.' He drew some notes from his pocket. 'I had a little win, didn't I now?'

Twenty pounds. A lot of use that would be. 'Why did you do it?' she pleaded. 'Surely now we've sorted things out Adam will . . . '

'Oh, your precious Adam isn't the only person in the world!'

She stiffened. 'What d'you mean?' His eyes evaded hers. 'Come on, you must tell me. Are you owing money to anyone else?'

Bonnie went to turn away, but she blocked him. Helplessly he lifted his arms, and let them flop to his side. 'It was when I owed the Owd Man so much. I got a loan . . . ' His voice tailed away.

'You went to a moneylender?' Maggie's eyes were dark with apprehension. 'Dear God! How much Da? How much do you owe him?'

He hung his head. 'Two thousand . . . or maybe three.'

She closed her eyes to stop the room from reeling. She had thought they were safe . . . and now this. And was it even the end of it? She wouldn't put it past her father to have more debts up his sleeve that he still hadn't mentioned. And still he didn't seem to understand the enormity of what he had done.

'Come on, Maggie,' he coaxed. 'Don't get mad at me. I'll get a big win one of these days, sure and I will. Anyway, when you're married to that nice young man you'll have plenty. There's no time to be cross with me now.'

She cast an agonized glance at the clock on the wall. He was right. In another quarter of an hour Adam would be arriving. 'If you want your

177

dinner it's in the oven,' she snapped. 'We'll have to talk about this some other time.' And she left him, before she said things in her anger that she would regret later.

She sorted through the clothes now hanging freshly pressed in her wardrobe, and picked a red silk dress. She had never felt less like going to a party . . . let alone her own engagement party. What a laugh that was! She felt sick with apprehension. This bombshell of her father's was the final straw. It had completely destroyed any hope she might have had of wriggling out of her agreement with Adam — and even if she did continue, the problem still remained. How were they going to pay this further debt? Pulling the dress over her head, she thought bitterly that her father was living in a fool's paradise. If he only knew that there was no possibility of a marriage taking place, he might not be taking things so lightly.

The beginnings of a headache began niggling somewhere behind her eyes.

Usually she wore very little make-up, but tonight was different; she would need every scrap of confidence it could give her, and so she applied eye liner to grey eyes that already looked as though they had been put in with a sooty finger, and used blusher on her high moulded cheekbones, while her mind strayed to other things. She had hoped her father would mend his ways now that she was home, but it was not that easy. Now the gambling bug had taken a firm hold there might be no stopping him — she had seen such things before. Perhaps Adam . . . but no. He was the last person to confide in, she was already painfully aware of how much she was in his debt. So what was she to do?

The beeping of a horn told her that Adam had arrived. Quickly she ran a comb through her hair, and left it flying loose, long and shining. No time to attempt anything more sophisticated now. In any case . . . what did it matter? What she looked like was of little importance compared with the troubles that were sitting on her shoulders like a dark cloud. 'I'm coming,' she called.

Adam was already at the door, casually dressed in cream slacks and a navy blazer. His pale blue shirt was open at the neck, showing smooth skin surprisingly brown for a businessman. To her annoyance Maggie found her eyes filling with tears at the sight of him. She fought down the desire to run and fling herself into his arms, letting him take care of everything. He could, she was sure of that. Adam could cope with anything . . . except perhaps his feelings for Irene.

He looked at her, and she felt that he could see her distress in spite of the brilliant smile she flashed at him.

'I hope I'm not too early?'

'Not at all. Are you ready Da? Have you eaten?'

'No need. No need. I had a bite at Mickey's place.' Bonnie grinned ingratiatingly. 'Sure, I'll have some when we get back. It smells a fine stew.' He turned to Adam. 'Maggie's a fine cook.'

'Is she, indeed? You're a creature of many talents, Maggie.'

She could see the laughter in his eyes, and flushed. 'If you've finished bletherin' Da, we'll be going.'

It didn't take them long to reach the local, known to everyone as 'Biddie's Place'. It may have had another name, years ago, but if so it had been long forgotten. It was a plain stone building, next to and part of the village store, managed by Biddie McBride, a large motherly woman with a waspish tongue and a heart as big as her body. There were already cars parked all along the road, and Maggie's heart sank at the thought of facing so many people. She hesitated outside the door, hearing the buzz of voices, and music already on the go inside. Adam put his arm around her shoulders.

'Ready, darling?'

For a moment she felt comforted. With his arm around her she would be able to face anything ... but the

181

protection was illusory. She looked at him scornfully, a bitter smile twisting her lips. 'Of course, dearest.'

'Remember what I said,' he warned, as he opened the door.

7

A great hullabaloo greeted their arrival, and they were drawn in to mingle with the crowd. The air was blue with cigarette smoke, and the noise was shattering. Her father must have invited everyone for miles around, thought Maggie, and wondered with a sinking feeling who was supposed to pay for all this.

'Maggie! Ah, bless you, congratulations . . . and to your fine man.'

She was enveloped in Biddie's warm embrace, and then Adam took his turn. Most of the people pressing forward to congratulate them were already known to him, workers on the estate, Father Donovan, young Jimmy Connor's parents, and Dr Flaherty — and Maggie introduced those who were strangers to him. They were no strangers to her though; she had known most of them since she was tiny, and she felt sick at the thought of the way she was fooling them.

'Over here, Maggie.' A hand waved from the corner.

'Who's that, darling?'

'It's the O'Leary brothers. They play at every function here-abouts ... have done for as long as I can remember.'

They worked their way over to the corner, where stools had been reserved for them close to the musicians, three old men as alike and wrinkled as three walnuts. Smiling broadly the O'Learys nodded and broke into a lively tune. Adam sat next to Maggie and, following the example of the others, began clapping in time to the music, as relaxed and pleased with life as if his pleasure was genuine. The whole thing was a nightmare. Across the room Maggie saw her father buying drinks for his cronies. Her headache increased ten-fold.

'Enjoying yourself, my sweet?' Adam's

murmur held a subtle warning.

She tossed back her hair, and raised her chin. 'Naturally — why wouldn't I be?' He could take that how he chose. Flashing him a smile which never reached her eyes, she joined in the accompaniment.

Drinks were brought for them; large glasses of Guinness, black, smooth and bitter-sweet, that slid down the throat and left a creamy moustache on the lips. As the evening wore on song followed song, and drink followed drink. Bonnie appointed himself Master of Ceremonies, and was lording it in grand style, extracting every bit of juice out of the importance of the occasion. There was nothing she could do about it, and soon even the headache was stunned into submission.

Once, when Adam was up at the bar, Tim O'Leary lay down his fiddle and leaned close to her.

'He's a good man,' he whispered.

She was sick of hearing that ... everyone had been telling her — and didn't she know it herself, deep down.

'I was thinking he might not be liked here,' she remarked. 'You know, being from England, and coming over here to run a business.'

'But isn't he the Owd Man's nephew?' objected Biddie who was collecting glasses. 'Sure and he's one of us at heart.'

When Adam returned he slid an arm around her, and she leaned against him, grateful for his support, her head resting against his shoulder. It was solid and reassuring against her cheek, and his fingers were beating a tattoo against her ribs. She gave a sigh of pleasure. it was too much effort even to wonder whether he was really enjoying himself as much as he appeared to be, or if this was just as false as everything else about him. Adam tucked in his chin, to look down thoughtfully at the crown of her head.

'Maggie — give us a dance,' somebody shouted.

She was jerked upright into wakefulness. 'Me? Oh no . . . it's been years.' She flushed.

Adam hugged her, grinning. 'Go on, love,' he urged. 'This I can't wait to see.'

'Let's have a jig,' called her father across the room.

Giving her no time to refuse, seats were scraped back and bodies pressed together to make a space. 'Remember this one,' piped up the oldest O'Leary brother, waving the bow of his fiddle at her, then he tucked the instrument under his chin, his eyes twinkling.

Reluctantly Maggie kicked off her shoes and stood in the centre of the circle. Embarrassed, her eyes sought Adam, and found his answering glance daring her. It was that infuriating look of amusement that goaded her. With a tilt of her chin she tossed back her dark mane of hair again, and began, arms relaxed at her sides, back erect, all the movement concentrated in her stockinged feet.

It had been many years since she had danced an Irish jig. Her mother had taught her all the old dances, and it was her mother she remembered with heart-rending clarity now, as the room spun around her. The skirt of her red dress flared, revealing smooth strong calves. It moulded the proud line of her body, chin up and shoulders back. As the music's speed increased she laughed, caught up in spite of herself in the exhilaration of it. She saw Adam joining in the clap-beats with the best of them, his face alight with enjoyment and something else . . . almost pride. Was that more of his play-acting? Faces flashed before her, smiling, approving . . . the insistent tempo of the fiddle, pipe and drum driving her on faster and faster, until her calf muscles ached, and she could scarcely catch her breath.

Then, as suddenly as it had started, it was over. Cheered and patted she was propelled back to her seat, while Biddie bustled forward with drinks for the musicians.

'You were wonderful,' said Adam as she reached him, but she made no response. She had seen her father deep in conversation with Mickey from the racetrack, and another man she remembered seeing before, and knew to be a heavy gambler. She felt perspiration break out on her forehead, and the room closed in on her.

Adam put out a hand to steady her. 'Are you all right?'

Was he making more plans for the races . . . her Da? He was already well away in drink, she could see that from his larger-than-life gestures and heightened colour.

'Maggie?' Adam's arm came around her waist. 'You need air. Hold on to me.' He elbowed his way through the crowd, drawing her behind him in the space he created, until they were outside, and he closed the door against the din. She leaned against the wall thankfully, conscious of the rough surface against her back, looking up at the bright pin points of the stars in the canopy of the sky.

'You'll catch a chill.' He slipped off his jacket and placed it around her, easing her arms into the sleeves as if she were a child, and buttoning it. 'You're hot from dancing.'

The coat still held the warmth of his body, and it awoke all the yearnings she had been stifling so resolutely. 'Did I make a fool of myself in there?' she asked. 'Did I embarrass you?'

He placed his hands on the wall either side of her head, his eyes unfathomable in the shadows, his mouth too close for comfort.

'You'll never do that, Maggie.'

She gave a half-smile. It was all very well for him to say so, but what Irene had said was right. He came from a very different world. She fought against the insidious wave of desire that rose in her, desire to lean her head forward and cross those few inches that would bring his firm mouth against hers; the knowledge that she could lose herself in his kiss; be cocooned against all her troubles, even though she knew they would return in sickening force when the evening was over. Adam made no move — but she felt he was waiting to see what she would do.

'You didn't invite your mother and Irene though,' she said deliberately, to break the spell.

He drew back, his arms dropping to his sides. He tilted his head, looking at her through eyes mere slits, his mouth tucked in. 'I did ask mother, but she felt it would be too strenuous for her. As for Irene . . . did you want her to come?' He knew very well she didn't, there was not even any need to answer. 'As a matter of fact,' he added slowly, 'I think Irene and I are coming to some sort of understanding. I need those shares, and I intend to get them.'

That was it then. Irene had not been lying. Maggie felt the energy draining out of her.

'Do you want to go back in?' he asked. 'They sound as if they're still enjoying themselves in there.'

She shook her head. 'Will you take me home please?' she asked in a small voice. 'I just can't take any more.'

'Sometimes second-best isn't so bad,' he said shortly. 'Just think about it, Maggie.'

Tears hot and heavy sprang into her eyes. He might be willing to use her as second best — as a substitute for Irene — but she knew it was not enough for herself. 'Just take me home.'

He shrugged. 'Here are the car keys. You can get in, while I explain to your father.'

By the time he returned she was huddled in his passenger seat. 'Is Da coming too?' she asked dully.

'I doubt if wild horses would drag your father away for hours yet,' he said drily. 'Don't worry. Someone will bring him home. And they're all too busy to miss us. In any case, they think it natural we want some time alone together.'

'That just goes to show how wrong

people can be,' she said wearily.

At the cottage he insisted on coming in with her. 'I've something to say,' he told her.

She looked at him, making no effort to disguise the pain she was feeling. The time was past when she could pass it off as a joke. But, strangely, it was not really Adam who was hurting her now . . . it was her father. She just did not know what to do. Her shoulders drooped, the eyes she turned on him were huge in her too-pale face.

'What is it then?'

'I'm . . . sorry.' His voice was strained. 'I'm so sorry, Maggie.'

She tried to still her whirling thoughts. 'Sorry? For what?'

'For this whole thing. I didn't realize what a strain I was putting you under. Let's forget it ever happened.'

Her eyes searched his face. Was this new development because of his agreement with Irene? 'D'you really mean that?' she faltered. 'You want to drop this sham engagement? But what about father's debt? What about . . . '

'Forget the damned debt! I wish I'd never told you about it. No more debt. Do you understand?'

She understood. It was clear enough. He and Irene had come to an arrangement. Irene had said Adam would do anything for Blairs of Devon. He did not need protection any more because he had capitulated. Ah well, his mother would be pleased.

'But — what shall I tell everyone?'

'I'll see to that,' he said harshly. 'I got you into this, and I'll do all the explaining.' He raised a hand and gently stroked the dark curtain of hair from her face. 'My mistake was that I didn't realize how much you loved him.'

Her forehead wrinkled. 'But of course I love him,' she exclaimed. 'With all his faults, he's my Da . . . '

'I'm not talking about him, woman!' he exploded. 'I mean that lover of yours.'

'Malcolm?' She was too confused to

do other than speak the truth. 'But I don't . . . '

'You've been at the end of your tether all night,' he said bitterly. 'Did you think I didn't see? And why — just because I kissed you today.'

'No!' she exclaimed. 'It wasn't anything to do with you, Adam. I was upset because of Da.' She turned her head away, to hide the shame she felt for her father — but Adam might as well know the sordid truth, now that it was no longer his concern. 'He owes more. Lots more . . . oh, God knows how much . . . to a moneylender.'

'Is that all!' He cupped her hand around her chin, and forced her to look at him.

'I . . . don't know,' she faltered. 'There may be others.'

'I don't mean that.' He took a deep breath. 'D'you know what I was thinking when you were dancing there tonight?' he asked hoarsely.

She shook her head, unnerved by the fire burning in his eyes, unable to turn her gaze away, afraid to hear what he was about to say.

'I thought . . . this gorgeous woman is mine, but only in name. I wanted you then Maggie, as I want you now.'

Without moving she found herself in his arms, returning the kisses he rained down on her, with a hunger all the greater for knowing it was futile. Oh yes, he wanted her, but he wanted Irene's shares more. But that didn't matter now. All that mattered was the soft touch of his mouth, nuzzling at her neck, his hands expertly reaching behind her, sliding the zip of her dress until it slipped from her shoulders to slither in a heap of scarlet around her feet.

'Beautiful,' he muttered, swinging her about, so that she leaned back on him while he slid his hands over the swelling silken cups of her bra, lifting the full ripeness of her breasts. 'Beautiful, splendid girl.'

'Ah . . . ' She could not help herself. She gave a small cry of pleasure as his lips teased their way down her neck to the pale skin of her shoulder, and she turned to press her lips against his hair.

'Not here,' she protested breathlessly.

Holding his hand, she led him up the narrow stairs to her room. Somewhere in the back of her mind a small voice insisted that she would be sorry and heartsore tomorrow, when Irene claimed him back for her own. But she had great difficulty in listening to that voice. This moment was all hers . . . that was all she could think about.

In the pale moonlight Adam laid her on the bed, and discarding his jacket stretched out beside her. She reached to undo his shirt, but he held her hands.

'Let me look at you.'

She arched her back to allow him to reach behind her and undo the clasp of her flimsy bra. She heard his sharp intake of breath, and felt her own tide of passion ride up as she lay proud and unashamed.

'You're so beautiful,' he whispered. 'You drive me mad!'

His lips fastened greedily on her neck, and he kissed his way down the long line of her throat, working his way to where the swelling orbs of her breasts were responding to the gentle stroking motions of his hands. She gasped his name as his mouth claimed first one and then the other rosy tip, until she was trembling with uncontrollable desire.

He rose to his knees, and she lifted her hips for him to remove the last vestige of lacy silk that hid her from him, as he bent to kiss her toes, his fingers warm under her instep. Then his hands stroked their way up her firm brown calves, up to the whiteness of her thighs . . .

It was more than she could bear. 'Please . . . ' she begged. 'Adam, I must touch you. Let me . . . '

He stood beside the bed, his fingers swiftly unfastening his shirt. It was light enough for her to see his eyes glittering with the reflection of her own passion. His shirt thrown aside, he stood magnificent, as she had known he would be — his broad swimmer's shoulders muscular, his chest only slightly shaded by a vee of fine dark hair. She reached up, and he bent over her, so that she was able to run her hands down his back. She pulled him against her, her lips sweet against his warm skin. Touching him lightly, in a daze of delight, she ran her hands across his ribs . . .

Then he stopped her, frozen in a listening attitude.

'What is it?' she whispered.

'Hush!'

There was a slam of a car door — voices — a car driving away, and then singing. Her father's singing.

'I don't believe it!' exclaimed Adam. 'Not again!'

Her soul cried out in revolt. It could not end like this. She had thought to have just this one night, before she lost Adam for ever . . . and her father had spoiled even that. And anyway, what was he doing back so soon? His voice

rose slurred and raucous from somewhere in the yard.

Have you ever seen the like, me boys,
Of Maloney's little cow.
She's the front legs of a kangaroo,
The back ones of a sow . . .

'I'll kill him,' said Adam in a
strangled voice, frustration mingling
with fierce laughter. 'So help me, I will!'

He struggled back into his shirt, and
tucked it in his trousers.

'My dress is downstairs,' Maggie
gasped, her face crimson. 'Oh . . . I feel
so stupid.'

He caught her face in his hands and
kissed her long and hard. 'On the
contrary, Maggie girl — you feel
delicious! Stay here! I'll get your dress.
He's not come in yet . . . though
goodness knows what he's doing out
there.'

He disappeared. From the yard came
a shattering roar.

'What's that?' she cried.

Adam bounded back up the stairs. 'Here's your dress. I'm going after him. He's drunk, and he's taken the tractor. If he ruins it, I'll . . . '

'Wait for me!' she shrieked. 'You'll need a torch.' Frantically she struggled into her dress and raced after him, but he had already gone, the cottage door was open. She shoved her feet into her gumboots, and grabbing the torch which always stood handy on the dresser, ran out into the darkness. 'Where are you?' she called.

'Here.' Adam loomed up. 'Listen . . . where's he heading?'

Maggie could hear the tractor's engine, receding. 'He's making for the potato field,' she decided. 'Come on.'

They ran, the beam from her torch bobbing about in front of them. When they turned into the open gateway to the field they could see tracks in the soft earth. Maggie caught Adam by the sleeve. 'Hush! Listen . . . he's near the bottom. He'll be crossing the logs.'

They pounded on after him. 'You're

ruining your shoes,' panted Maggie.

'That's the least of my worries! Stop
. . . what's happening now?'

As they stood gasping for breath they
heard the noise of the engine change. It
revved — roared — and then there was
a crashing sound . . . and silence.
Nothing could be heard, except a subtle
change in the burbling voice of the
stream.

'God . . . he's gone over the edge,'
said Adam. He began to run all out,
and Maggie raced after him, afraid to
think, afraid to imagine —

Her torch caught the shape of the
tractor. It was on its side in the stream.

'Da!' she screamed.

Adam reached it first. 'Maggie
. . . shine the torch.'

They found Bonnie in the stream.
Maggie plunged into the water. It was
icy, but she hardly felt it as she cradled
her father's head. His shoulders were
wedged against a rock, his eyes closed.

'He's pinned by his chest,' panted
Adam. He had his shoulders up against

the tractor's cab, straining to lift it. 'If I can move it, Maggie, can you pull him out?'

'You'll never lift that,' she sobbed. 'Adam . . . you'll have to go for help. But hurry, the tractor's acting like a dam. The water's rising. Take the torch.'

'No . . . you keep that. I can see well enough. Just keep his head up. I'll be as quick as I can.'

Then he was gone, and she was left in the darkness with her father. She squatted in the water, gripping his sodden coat, his head on her knees. She shone the torch on his face; He was breathing . . . but for how long? The water was so cold . . . it was up to his shoulders. How long would it take Adam to reach his car? There was no phone at the cottage . . . he'd have to drive to the Big House. Bonnie moaned.

'Da?'

He opened his eyes. 'Maggie?'

'Da . . . you'll be all right now. Adam's gone for help.'

He smiled. 'Did you see my new tractor?' he whispered. 'Sure, and isn't it a beauty?' He coughed.

'Don't talk Da.' She held him closer to her, laying her cheek against his wet hair . . . but she could not protect him from the muddy gurgling cold of the water that plucked at them both, as she crouched numbly, now waist-deep.

'I'll try it out in the morning,' he murmured. 'Your Ma will be so pleased . . . ' His eyes closed.

Hours later, it seemed, she heard the voices. From down the field lights came bobbing. There was shouting; the noise of vehicles. Adam reached her first, holding aloft a lantern that cast a garish yellow light over the whole scene. He plunged into the water.

'Not long now, Maggie girl. We'll soon have him out.'

She turned her head slowly towards him. Her face, caught in the circle of light, was blank . . . expressionless.

'It's no use,' she whispered. 'He's gone, Adam. Da's dead.'

8

On the day of the funeral it rained from the first crack of a grey dawn to an equally grey evening. Maggie stood in the kitchen at Ballybrae. It was becoming dark now, but she could see runnels of rain trickling down the window pane. They reminded her of the night she had arrived here, only a short while ago, and yet it seemed an age. So much had happened.

She could see herself reflected in the window — black skirt and plain grey blouse, the nearest she would bring herself to wearing mourning — although it was still expected of her here. She could see her face, eyes smudged with shadows. Behind her was the kitchen, dishes stacked waiting to be washed, the teapot waiting to be replenished. Ah yes . . . that was what she had come out for . . .

Like an automaton she filled the kettle. The mourners were drinking in the other room, Bonnie's friends from far and wide. Guinness and whiskey mainly. 'A fine do' Da would have called it, but the women folk preferred tea to wash down the slices of cold ham and beef, the pickles, the salads, the thinly sliced bread and butter, the tiny decorated fairy cakes, and the rich fruit cake.

She could hear the hum of voices, people enjoying themselves as only they knew how to enjoy a funeral — with a proper relish. To do less would be showing a lack of respect to the departed. And they *did* respect her father, in a funny kind of way. With a spurt of heightened noise the kitchen door opened, and Mrs Murphy pushed her way through, arms full of a tray of empties.

'There you are, then. Are you all right, my dear?'

'Yes . . . of course.' Maggie's smile was mechanical. She had been smiling it all day, and it came and went as required without her hardly noticing it. She placed the kettle on the cooker, and turned the flame up high. With an effort she focussed on the older woman.

'It . . . was good of you to help out. I really am grateful.'

There was a mixture of pity and exasperation on Mrs Murphy's angular features. She moved forward, the tray held out.

'Can you make room for these? There . . . that's fine.' Her hands free she patted Maggie on the shoulder. 'You know, you're not really fit for this. You should have stayed in bed a few days more.'

Maggie shook her head, her lips taking on a stubborn line. 'There's nothing wrong with me. Truly! And I couldn't put the funeral off any longer — it was delayed enough as it was.'

Mrs Murphy sniffed. 'Not surprising. It's a wonder you weren't worse, soaking wet and cold to the bone when they brought you back. Dr Flaherty said you nearly had pneumonia.'

'But I'm all right now.'

'That you're not!'

'Look,' said Maggie, 'I'm sure they need you in there. I'll bring in the tea as soon as it's ready.'

'You should have had the funeral from the Big House,' persisted Mrs Murphy. 'Then we could have looked after you properly. Mrs Blair wanted you to . . . '

'No!' Maggie broke in vehemently, and then quieter, 'Da would have wanted to go from his own home, as mother did, not from a stranger's . . . though it was kind of Mrs Blair.'

'Well . . . ' Mrs Murphy hesitated. 'If you're sure you are all right, I'd better go back in.' She picked up a plate of sandwiches, and disappeared again, much to Maggie's relief.

They had all worried too much, she thought wearily. Mrs Blair in particular had been surprisingly kind, whisking her away into a hot bath the moment Adam had taken her to the

Big House. It had been Mrs. Blair who had nursed her through those first few bad days, when she hardly knew where she was or — mercifully — what had happened.

And Adam too, of course. He had been there in the background all the time, taking everything upon his own shoulders, all the worry of the post mortem, the police enquiries, the funeral arrangements. And Da's debts too. Miraculously that knotty problem had somehow disappeared. Some day soon she would have to ask him . . . but not yet. He had stood by her side at Bonnie's grave too, head bowed in the pouring rain. He was in the other room now, ready to stand between her and the weight of sympathy that threatened to engulf her.

The kettle started to boil and Maggie tipped its contents into the fat brown teapot she had had to borrow from Biddie's kitchen. Continuing her line of thought she reflected with a wry smile that Adam was, to all intents and purposes, still her fiancé. On that terrible night he had promised to release her, but her father's death had changed all that. How could she keep him to that promise, at the present moment? It would look so bad, and though the people round about had taken him to their hearts, he would soon lose their respect if they thought he had treated her badly. She could not do that to him. No . . . there would have to be a decent interval. In the meantime, she would make things easier by finding some excuse to leave. Some urgent business in London, perhaps. Adam would need the cottage in any case, to lease to another tenant who would carry on working the land her father had loved. Ah yes . . . he *had* loved it.

The tea having stood for the required time, she began filling the cups and placing them on the tray. She had brought out her mother's best china for the occasion, but had had to borrow more. Two of the rose patterned cups had disappeared, she noticed, and one of the plates was chipped. She had intended replacing them . . .

When she joined the others the noise hit her like a solid wall. Adam saw her wince, and was immediately at her side. 'Can you cope?'

She gave him the same automatic smile. 'Don't worry.' She began handing round the cakes, but Jimmy Connor's mother took the plate from her hand, and Father Donovan drew her to one side. A friend of the family for as long as she could remember, even though she had not attended his church herself, he was a kindly and practical man.

'You're being very brave, Maggie,' he told her with approval. 'But I know how you are feeling.'

'Do you?' She doubted it.

'You must console yourself,' continued the priest, 'with the thought that Bonnie never suffered. Never suffered at all, the doctor says.' He patted her shoulder. 'Perhaps — and you'll forgive me for saying this, my child — perhaps it was the Lord's way of knowing what was best for him.'

He was right, of course. How long could her father have continued, the way he was going? But it didn't make things any easier.

'Thank you, Father,' she replied. 'I'll try to think of that.'

'Good girl. Good girl — you're bearing up well.'

She busied herself with clearing spent plates. She was *not* bearing up well, she decided with icy clarity. She was just not feeling at all. Not grief . . . not pain . . . not anger . . . not shock. Just a grey numbness, as blank as the sheets of rain that had fallen on the overturned earth of her father's grave.

At last, and almost together as though there was an unwritten law about such things, people began to leave. In dribs and drabs they trickled away, and she stood by the door of the cottage like an automaton, shaking their hands, making the right responses. At last only those from the Big House were left.

'I'll stay and help you clear up,' offered Mrs Murphy.

Adam's mother stopped her. 'No . . . that can wait until the morning. We can send someone down then. The girl is nearly out on her feet. Take her home, Adam, and look after her.' Maggie did not argue. It did not seem worthwhile.

At the Big House Irene was waiting in the hall looking bored and irritable. She made a bee line for Adam. 'I was wondering when you'd be back. It's been hopeless here today. There's been nobody about to do anything. No-one to talk to.' Her voice trailed on, petulantly insistent. 'The surveyor wants to go over my house tomorrow. Will you come with me? Say you will, darling, I need your opinion too.'

Irene was the only one whose welcome to Maggie had been less than warm. She had constantly dragged Adam away on every opportunity, and he had spent a great deal of time with her. There had been days when he had disappeared for hours, ostensibly to look at the house his ex-wife had chosen, or to accompany her to the solicitors. Maggie shrugged her shoulders. Well . . . she need not worry. Soon Irene would have the field to herself, and then Adam would be sure of the shares he needed. The sight of them together did not even hurt any more. But even that was frightening, because it should . . . it should . . .

'Adam can discuss that with you later,' said Mrs Blair somewhat sharply. There had been signs lately that she was becoming less sympathetic to her ex daughter-in-law.

Irene wound her arms around Adam's neck. 'See that you do,' she murmured. 'It's time you had a little relaxation. You know, darling, you spend too much time worrying about other people.'

Maggie knew the barb was meant for her, but it did not matter. She did not wait to hear Adam's response, but turned away and slowly climbed the broad staircase to the room that had become hers. It was a pleasant room, the walls papered in a tiny leaf motif, the carpet and bedspread sage green to match the long velvet curtains, but to Maggie it was sufficient that it was a place of refuge from eyes that demanded more than she could give. What did they want? Signs of grief? If so, they must be very disappointed. It must be there, she acknowledged that. Some day it would surface, and that would be a good thing — but at this moment it was lying cold and heavy inside her, and all she wanted was to find oblivion in sleep.

She removed her shoes, placing them neatly side by side under the small button-backed chair that stood near the window. She drew the curtains together, and then removed her skirt and blouse, placing them carefully on a hanger. For some reason it seemed highly important that every action should be performed carefully, slowly and neatly.

When she had done that she stood, barefoot and clad only in her undies. She had chosen her plainest today, she thought, and her lips twisted in the travesty of a smile. Not that it mattered in the slightest, but it seemed only proper. She stood still, puzzling, unable to decide what she was supposed to do next.

'Maggie.'

She had not noticed him enter the bedroom. She did not even stop to ask herself what his mother would say, if she knew. She simply stood like a puzzled child, unable to make any move of her own, and when he took over — sliding her slip up over her head with gentle sure hands — she lifted her arms for him, in unquestioning obedience.

'It's been a long day,' he said, his voice deep and warm. 'It's late. Time for you to sleep.'

That brought a response. 'I can't sleep.'

He raised his lids, and his hazel eyes studied her face. 'Rest then,' he said laconically.

Somewhere in the back of her mind, it struck her that he was not being very sympathetic.

'I can't rest,' she explained, in the same blank voice.

He drew down the green coverlet, and the soft duvet, and then returned to her. She was still standing exactly as he had left her. He shook his head, and then took her by her arms.

'Turn around.'

She turned, and he undid her bra and removed it. She was aware of his action, but felt nothing. She thought she heard him sigh, but then he moved his hands down to her hips, slid his fingers into the waistband of her briefs and peeled them down, until they were around her ankles. 'Move your foot out. Now that one. Good girl.'

Then he lifted her bodily, and laid her on the bed. Drawing the covers up over her, he looked down and smoothed the hair from her forehead. Then he bent and kissed her gently. 'Try to get some sleep. It will help. Goodnight Maggie.' He moved towards the door and reached up to put out the light.

He was leaving her! At last something pierced the fog. 'Adam!'

The panic in Maggie's voice was clear to him. He turned.

'I'm cold,' she whispered, in a voice barely audible.

He walked back to the bed, and touched her cheek. 'You've no fever. Shall I bring you a hot water bottle?'

She shook her head imperceptibly. The duvet was pulled up to her chin, her hair a tumbled mass of black on the white pillow, and her eyes were nearly as dark as the fanned out strands as she turned to him. Her mouth moved, desperately striving for words that would convey the terror of the emptiness that was gripping her.

'It's not that kind of cold. I can't feel anything. Not *anything*!' Her voice rose. 'I feel like stone inside. It's as if . . . as if I had died, instead of Da.'

He took her hand, and her fingers curled convulsively around his. 'What is the matter with me?' she whispered. 'I can't cry. I don't feel any grief. I don't feel anything at all. I just seem . . . blank. As if I had nothing left inside. I can't stand it any longer. Adam . . . Don't go. Don't leave me alone tonight . . . please!'

For one dreadful moment she thought he was going to refuse, but then, without a word, he began pulling his shirt over his head. 'I won't leave you, Maggie, if that's what you want,' he said at last.

He had misunderstood her. All she wanted from him was comfort, to feel him near her, to draw on his warmth, to fend away the dark blankness that was engulfing her. 'Adam!' she gasped, 'I'm sorry . . . I don't want . . . '

'I know,' he said calmly. There was a slight quirk to the corners of his mouth, but his eyes were gentle.

She watched, mesmerized, as he sat

on the edge of the bed and began taking off his shoes and socks. She reached out a tentative hand, and touched his back. His skin was smooth and warm, and she ran her fingers down his spine, fascinated by the play of muscles that rippled as he moved. Then he stood up, looking down at her impassively, as he undid his belt. Without any embarrassment, trousers and briefs followed the shirt onto the floor.

'Move over, Maggie girl,' he said in a matter-of-fact tone, as he turned off the light and drew back the curtains. 'I'm coming in.'

He slid into the bed beside her, and she reached for him, hungrily accepting the warmth of his body against hers. She felt nothing for him as a man — that seemed to have died with the rest of her feelings — but he was alive. He was warm, and vibrant and vital. She nestled into him with a sigh of relief, and he eased an arm under her, so that her head slid onto his shoulder, and there seemed nowhere to put her own arm except around his waist.

'Thank you, Adam.'

There was a rumble in his chest that seemed to be a chuckle. 'You're more than welcome,' he said.

The darkness inside her began to recede, just a little. His shoulder was warm under her cheek, and she became aware that he smelled good. Experimentally, she moved her lips against his neck, and ran her tongue against his skin. He tasted slightly salty.

'Watch it!' he rumbled. 'Don't try me too hard, Maggie.'

He didn't need to warn her, she had felt the leaping response of his body, and somewhere deep in the cold reaches of the dead thing she had become, an answering flame began to flicker. With a little grunt of satisfaction she nuzzled closer into his arms. One of her hands was imprisoned, tucked somewhere in the space between them, but with her free hand she began tracing the line of his ribs.

'Damn you, Maggie — I'm trying to play the gentleman!'

He placed the flat of his hand between her shoulder blades, and slid it down her back, stroking her down all her length to the swelling curve of her hips, cupping his hand over one firm buttock.

'You're quite a handful . . . I'll say that for you!'

He made her laugh, and the darkness receded even further, the flame gaining strength. She moved her lips to the hard line of his jaw, and he turned his head to meet her. His mouth caught hers, imprisoning it, then releasing it again, only to capture her lips once more — playing with them, savouring their fullness, teasing her by withdrawing at the first sign of any response. At last, with a whimper of protest, she strained to reach his mouth and keep it. His kiss deepened, his hands tightened, and her bones melted as the darkness inside her surrendered at last, and fled before the fire that had begun to burn in her blood.

Just as she felt her senses reeling from the heady taste of his mouth, he moved again, fastening his lips on the hollow at the base of her throat. He pushed back the bed covers, and she felt the air cool on her skin — but she was not cold now. She felt feverish, with a burning need ... and still he restrained her. He dealt with her gently, exploring her body with his mouth and his strong warm hands, until her senses turned inwards to the need he had awoken but seemed determined not to assuage. Everything else was, for the moment, forgotten — gladly forgotten — in the rushing golden flame of the passion that engulfed her.

Suddenly he rolled her onto her back, imprisoning her hands on the pillows, either side of her head. In the pale light that fell across the bed from the window, she could just discern his features, but she could not see his expression.

'What . . . do you want of me?' she whispered.

'Everything,' he told her, his voice taut with desire. 'Everything . . . if you are willing to give it, Maggie.'

'Let me go,' she pleaded.

Slowly, reluctantly, he removed his hands and rose away from her, kneeling beside her, his eyes dark pools of shadow, his body tense, uncertain.

Now free, she sat up and cupped his face in her hands, tenderly. He had known her need, better even than she had known it, selflessly setting out to break the bonds the trauma of her father's death had forged. But in rescuing her he had woken a hunger in himself, that was now consuming him. She could feel it, hear it in his ragged breathing, as he knelt immobile beside her, waiting . . .

'I'm willing,' she whispered.

Her arms received him gladly. This might be the only time she would know the rapture of belonging to him . . . and she was not going to turn him away.

He lowered himself against her with a moan of delight. 'Maggie . . . oh, Maggie.'

She received him with answering abandon, drawing him closer to her, wanting to envelop him, to possess him now . . . while she had this one chance . . . while he was still hers. The flame flared out of all control, searing her whole body, fuelled by the rhythm of his possession. She gasped with the delight of it, almost wanting to beg him to stop. It was too much . . . she could not bear it . . .

His skin slick and hot against her own, he was muttering incoherent words, driving her with him further and further to a crescendo that was so frightening in its intensity that for a moment she held back. But it was too late . . . and together they were swept to a place where no time existed for them, until — it seemed aeons later — they lay, at peace in each other's arms.

After a while Adam reached down and pulled the duvet up over them.

'Not cold now?' he murmured, his voice lazy.

Maggie drew a shuddering breath. 'No — not now.'

The icy numbness that had gripped her since the night by the stream had gone but, in its melting, sensation had returned like life returning to hands once bitten by frost, and like them . . . it hurt. A tear trickled down her cheek, fast followed by another.

'I'm sorry,' she choked. 'Adam . . . it's not you. It's just . . . '

'I know,' he comforted. 'Cry all you need. It's right that you should. It's all right Maggie. You're safe now.'

Yes — even as she clung to him in her paroxysm of grief, she knew she was safe with him — for this night at least — and because of him she had been set free to grieve for her father, and let him go, remembering him with love, and learning to live without him.

At last her tears were spent, and Adam dried her eyes.

'You must sleep now,' he told her,

and turned her gently onto her side, cuddling up behind her, his arm heavy across her waist.

'Goodnight Maggie,' he murmured, kissing the back of her neck.

She yawned, a delicious jaw-aching yawn. 'Goodnight Adam.' And almost before she had finished saying his name, she drifted into a dreamless sleep.

9

She woke up the next morning, early, and stretched out an arm. It encountered nothing. She turned her head, but Adam was not there, only a depression in the pillow beside her showed where his head had lain. The bed on his side still felt warm. He had not been gone for long, and she knew just where he would be — down at his swimming pool. She had been in this house long enough to know that Adam went there first thing every morning, without fail — and that was where he would have gone now, creeping out silently for fear of disturbing her.

She rolled over, and laid her cheek against his pillow. Recollections of the previous day flooded into her mind. What a strange day it had been, and how people would be shocked if they knew what had happened. But people would be wrong to think badly of either of them. What had happened had been an act of compassion on Adam's part even though he had left her in no doubt that it had been just as shattering an experience for him as it had been for herself. But the difference was . . . she loved him.

Her lips quivered, and she pressed them against the soft linen, seeking for an echo of the contact of his body. He had comforted her . . . but for him his business was all-important. For that he had already given in to Irene's demands. And so there was only one thing for her to do. If she loved him she must prove it. She must willingly give him back to Irene, and hope that with her he would find happiness. She must leave, and as quickly as possible.

She stifled a sob. This was no time to feel sorry for herself. At least she had one precious memory to keep with her always, and that was more than many people had in a lifetime. She swung her legs out of the bed, and stood up, stretching. Her limbs felt stiff, and she warmed at the recollection of the abandonment that had caused such stiffness. She would go to him now, she thought. Now, before her nerve failed her. She would thank him for the gift of life he had given to her . . . and tell him that she was leaving.

She only stopped long enough to slip on her dressing gown, a blue silk wrap-around affair that had seen better days and barely covered her knees, and left her room, her hair still tousled, her feet bare. It would not matter. Nobody was likely to be about at this hour, other than Adam himself. But there she was wrong. She had forgotten that there was one other person who had come to know Adam's habits equally well, and who was determined to take advantage of the fact.

Maggie let herself into the large empty space of the conference room and saw that the curtains at the far end were pulled slightly apart and one of the glass doors to the pool had been slid aside. Proof of Adam's passage through, she thought, and she stepped gladly forward to find him. But it was not Adam who was lounging in one of the brightly coloured chairs beside the pool, but Irene. She too was dressed in a wrap, a frothy creation of white lace that made her appear more delectably feminine than ever.

When she saw Maggie she looked decidedly annoyed. A scowl marred the perfection of her features, perfection carefully arranged, Maggie noticed, seeing the artfully blended colour around the green eyes that stared so balefully at her. Even the long eyelashes, she hazarded a guess, were false. Nobody could have eyelashes so thick and long!

'If you're looking for Adam, he's in the changing room,' Irene said curtly. She rose in one fluid movement, and sauntered towards Maggie, looking her up and down in undisguised contempt. 'Couldn't you sleep?'

'No,' said Maggie, seizing the excuse

with relief. 'No . . . I couldn't.' It was as well the other did not know where Adam had spent the night, she thought with a shiver.

Irene noticed the involuntary movement. 'You'd better get back to bed before you catch another chill. The last thing Adam needs is to have *you* on his hands any longer than he has to. Can't you see he's only looking after you out of pity?' She bent down and trailed long fingers in the water that lapped the blue ceramic tiles at the edge of the pool.

In spite of her determination to remain calm, Maggie felt her ire rising. 'You needn't worry,' she said flatly. 'I'm leaving today.'

Irene looked up sharply. 'Oh . . . really?' She rose to her feet once more. 'I think you're being very sensible,' she said silkily. 'The whole position here must be very awkward for you, living on charity, so to speak. Now — if I were you I'd disappear before Adam returns. I won't tell him you've been here pestering him again . . . after all, the poor man *is* entitled to some privacy, you know . . . and we want to enjoy our swim without spectators.'

'Are you going to swim then?' asked Maggie sceptically.

'Why yes,' answered Irene. 'I'm all prepared.' She opened her wrap, revealing the skimpiest bikini Maggie had ever seen. Irene seemed to have been poured into it, and small she might be, but she was nevertheless extremely shapely. Maggie doubted if the woman intended to get that bikini wet . . . it looked more like man-bait to her!

'Adam and I meet down here every morning,' Irene purred. 'It's so intimate here, don't you think?' She snuggled back into her wrap, confident now, triumphant, seeing that she'd got what she wanted. But would she keep her bargain with Adam?

'Have you signed over those shares yet?' Maggie asked bluntly.

Irene looked amused. 'Not yet. I'm not a complete idiot, you know. Adam will get what he wants, on the day we are re-married.'

So that was it. Marriage had been the condition Adam had agreed to, and for this he had crept from her bed to meet Irene here. Perhaps if she had not begged him to stay he would have spent the night with Irene too. Maggie burned with anger — disappointment too, that he should have been willing to sacrifice himself this way, simply for the sake of his business. She had thought better of him.

Irene tapped her foot, impatiently. 'Well — go if you're going. Don't you know you're not wanted here?'

'I *am* going,' cried Maggie, colour flooding into her face, her eyes bright with the anger she had been holding down. 'But before I go I'll tell you this, Mrs Manson. You are the most despicable, evil woman I've ever met. You may think you have won, but you won't ever be happy. It will be a hollow victory, because you'll destroy Adam!'

'How dare you speak to me like that!' Disbelief on Irene's face turned to vindictiveness. 'Don't talk to me of hurting Adam. What have you and your precious father done but cause him trouble?' She stood right in front of Maggie, sneering. 'I know all about it, you know. It's cost Adam dear, looking after you and paying off the debts of a pathetic drunken old sot . . . '

'You . . . you little bitch!' gasped Maggie. In her distress she hardly knew what she did. All she wanted was to shut that vicious mouth and the things it was saying about her Da. 'Oh . . . go and have your damned swim!'

A good shove, and Irene was flying backwards, her mouth open in surprise — but as she went she caught hold of Maggie's wrap, and she was jerked off her feet too. They both tumbled together, in one almighty splash. Maggie didn't care. They both went under, and rose together. Maggie grabbed Irene's shoulders and dunked her under once more. 'Don't you ever speak of my father like that!' she spluttered.

Irene came up gasping. The blonde curls were plastered flat to her head — a narrow rat-shaped little head, it now turned out to be — and down the streaming cheeks slid what looked like two black spiders. Maggie stared closer . . . yes, she had been right, those eyelashes had definitely been false. She began to laugh.

'You're . . . you're mad,' choked Irene. She started to struggle to the side of the pool, her white wrap floating around her like a great deflated balloon. 'Wait until I tell Adam,' she shrilled. 'You're crazy. Thank heavens you're going . . . '

Maggie plunged after her, and grasping her by the shoulder, swung her round. 'Well, you needn't sound so pleased. Because I've changed my mind.' She threw back her dripping hair, sending a cascade of droplets over them both. She felt free — in a kind of exultation. She was not going to leave

Adam in Irene's clutches ... no, by God she was not ...

'What d'you mean?' cried Irene, splashing frantically in her effort to escape. 'You promised ... '

'That was before you really showed what a nasty bit of goods you are,' said Maggie scornfully. 'D'you think I would really let Adam ruin his life by marrying you? *I love him*! D'you hear that Irene? *I love him*. You wouldn't understand the meaning of the word.' As always, under strong emotion, the Irish in her voice grew stronger. 'So you can take yourself off and leave my fiancé alone, so you can — or I'll give you another ducking, and maybe keep you under next time!'

She had no real intention of carrying out her threat, but Irene obviously thought otherwise. With a shriek she tore herself loose and plunged to the side, hampered by her sodden robe. 'You've done it now!' she spat out as she reached the steps. 'Adam can whistle for his shares. I never meant him to have them, anyway.'

'How interesting,' said a deep voice.

They had been too engrossed to notice Adam's arrival, but he was there now. He was ready for his morning's swim, dressed only in the briefest of black bathing trunks that emphasized his muscular legs beneath slender hips, and his magnificently powerful frame. He stretched forward, holding out a hand to Irene, and when she grasped it he lifted her bodily out of the pool.

'Thank God you're here,' she cried. 'That . . . that creature attacked me!'

'So I noticed,' he answered briefly, and his eyes were cold.

Maggie swallowed hard and turned to the other side of the pool, unable to bear the condemnation in his eyes.

'Stay where you are,' he ordered, pointing a stern finger, and she stopped, the water lapping around her shoulders.

'Is that all you have to say to her?' demanded Irene, fuming. 'Tell her to go, Adam. Throw her out. You owe it to me . . . '

'*I owe you nothing.*'

He towered over the figure dripping before him, menacing. 'I've put up with you around here for purely business reasons, Irene, but don't think I didn't know what your game was. I haven't forgotten how you left me when you thought Charles was a better bet . . . and how you destroyed my child to do it.'

Maggie gasped, rooted to the spot, her eyes turning from one to the other of them, but they seemed oblivious of her presence.

'It was so long ago . . . ' began Irene.

'It's not something a man forgets,' interrupted Adam with a bitter laugh. 'You were already carrying my child when you set your cap at Charles. You realized a baby had no place in his plans, and so you got rid of it. Without telling me. Without caring what I thought. *You killed my child, damn you!*'

'I was ill,' she faltered.

'Only because things went wrong. You brought that on yourself. You got all the sympathy you needed from Charles. Don't expect any from me.'

'But these last few days you let me think you wanted . . .'

'I wanted a transport company. That was *all* I wanted from you, Irene.'

She stared at him, pale with disbelief, then she bared her teeth in a snarl. 'Well, you'll never get it now,' she hissed. 'Never!'

Gathering her dripping garments around her she fled, leaving Maggie clutching the side of the pool, shaken by the scene she had just witnessed. Adam watched his ex-wife disappear, and then turned his gaze.

'And now,' he said in an alarmingly quiet voice, 'having successfully ruined my takeover bid . . . it's your turn.'

He dived into the pool, cleaving the water cleanly without even a splash. Maggie waited for him to reappear, but he did not surface. She peered nervously down at the pool's surface, trying ineffectually to push down her blue wrap that floated up around her waist.

'Adam,' she faltered. 'Where are you?'

He erupted from beneath her, bursting up from under her wrap, his hands clasping her bare hips.

She was swept off her feet, his arms propelling her upwards until she shot out of the water. 'Adam!' she shrieked. 'Stop it.'

He let her down, sliding her through his arms and down his chest, his skin abrasive against hers, sliding until their bodies were welded together, and he was looking down at her, his mouth tucked in, his hooded eyes as impassive as ever.

'What am I to do with *you*?' he asked.

She took a deep breath. 'I'm not sorry for what I did. I can't pretend I am.'

'I believe you. Just look at you

— cheeks flushed, eyes sparkling, your fine black hair like a waterfall down your back. You look like an avenging water nymph, Maggie Nolan. You've thoroughly enjoyed yourself.'

'Yes,' she said defiantly. 'I have. And I'd do it again, if I had to. But, I'm sorry about the shares. Will it matter very much?'

'I'll have to abandon the takeover,' he said shortly.

'Oh . . .'

She did not know what to say to him. She had ruined everything — all the plans he had been so carefully preparing for months past — and yet she still was not sorry. He would never have been happy with Irene. It couldn't have worked, and if he was angry with her, so be it.

He lifted her out of the water and sat her on the edge of the pool, climbing out beside her. 'Take off your robe,' he ordered, picking up a large towel that was hanging over the back of a chair. When she obeyed he wrapped its fluffiness around her, and swung her up into his arms. 'We'll finish this conversation upstairs,' he said.

'But Adam,' Maggie protested, as he carried her through the house, her hair trailing over his arm leaving a track of drips behind them, 'What if your mother sees us?'

'Mother is quite a liberated spirit,' he answered with an amused smile. 'And she likes you.'

He saw her surprised expression. 'Oh yes she does,' he continued. 'And she's learned a bit more about Irene — things I should perhaps have told her long ago, but could not bring myself to.'

They reached her room, and he carried her inside and shut the door. Then standing her back on her feet, he unwrapped the towel and rubbed dry her hair, and on down to dry the rest of her. 'You've a fine body, my Maggie,' he said appreciatively.

She took the towel from him and smiled into his eyes. 'You're not so bad yourself!'

She took her turn then, drying him, taking pleasure in rubbing the firm long back, reaching up on her toes to towel his shoulders, kneeling to smooth those muscled legs with the dark hairs flattened damp on the skin.

'You'll have to work hard to catch up with the typing,' he said suddenly. 'The dictation has piled up.'

She looked up, startled. Was that all he wanted of her, to be his secretary again? Surely he must know by now that she could not settle for that . . .

Then she saw he was smiling, teasing. She gave a low laugh, and leaned against him, rubbing her cheek languorously against his thigh. He reached down and stroked her hair, already curling, its tendrils twining around his fingers.

'Are you cold, Maggie?'

She understood his meaning. 'I . . . am rather,' she whispered.

He lifted her back into the bed, covering them both with the soft voluminous duvet. 'We can't have that,' he murmured. He lay, supported on his elbows, looking down into her eyes, smoothing her hair away from her face. 'You realize you'll have to make an honest man of me now?' he told her.

Maggie's eyes were full of trust. 'And what d'you mean by that?'

'You're going to marry me.'

'Is that an order, sir?'

'It is.'

'Then, naturally, I'll have to obey.'

He smiled, rubbing a finger over her full lips, as he had that other time . . . oh, it seemed so long ago now. 'You did mean what you said to Irene? About loving me?'

'Don't you know?'

He shrugged. 'I thought you were hankering after Malcolm.'

He had got the name right at last. 'I never really loved him,' she said. 'I've known that for a long time.' She reached up and touched his face, wonderingly. 'I thought you considered me second best.'

He laughed. 'You! Never. Right from

the moment I met you, Maggie, I knew. You said marriage was important. That was what I liked about you — your strength, your honesty.'

She lowered her eyes. 'I thought perhaps, your business was more important.'

He shook his head. 'Leprechaun's gold, Maggie. I've learned that. Without you it means nothing. This . . . what we have . . . is the real thing.'

He lowered his lips to her, but she pushed him away. 'Will you say it then?'

He knew what she wanted. 'I love you, Maggie Nolan. I always will.'

Then he would brook no more resistance. He took her lips, as he had already taken her heart, and she opened to him as the flowers in the meadows open to the morning sun. Last night he had thawed the icy wastes of her soul, but today those wastes had blossomed, and she met him, kiss for kiss, heart to heart, knowing at last that there was no need for reservation, no need to fear. For a brief moment she heard her Da's voice saying, 'He's a fine man, indeed he is.'

'You're right there,' she whispered in the secret corners of her mind, before the passion that swept them both carried her away. Then there was no more thinking, no more wondering . . . only the certainty of his arms, and the knowledge of his love. A love, she knew, that would last for all time.

THE END

CONVALESCENT HEART

Lynne Collins

They called Romily the Snow Queen, but once she had been all fire and passion, kindled into loving by a man's kiss and sure it would last a lifetime. She still believed it would, for her. It had lasted only a few months for the man who had stormed into her heart. After Greg, how could she trust any man again? So was it likely that surgeon Jake Conway could pierce the icy armour that the lovely ward sister had wrapped about her emotions?

TOO MANY LOVES

Juliet Gray

Justin Caldwell, a famous personality of stage and screen, was blessed with good looks and charm that few women could resist. Stacy was a newcomer to England and she was not impressed by the handsome stranger; she thought him arrogant, ill-mannered and detestable. By the time that Justin desired to begin again on a new footing it was much too late to redeem himself in her eyes, for there had been too many loves in his life.